D0093206

# PEMBERLEY

ALSO BY EMMA TENNANT

The Bad Sister
The Adventures of Robina
Two Women of London: The Strange Case of Ms Jekyll and
  Mrs Hyde
Faustine
Tess

# PEMBERLEY

## A Sequel to Pride and Prejudice

## Emma Tennant

Hodder & Stoughton
LONDON SYDNEY AUCKLAND

British Library Cataloguing in Publication Data

Tennant, Emma
  Pemberley
  I. Title
  823.914 [F]

ISBN 0-340-59881-6

Published by Hodder and Stoughton,
a division of Hodder and Stoughton Ltd,
Mill Road, Dunton Green, Sevenoaks, Kent TN13 2YA
Editorial Office: 47 Bedford Square, London WC1B 3DP

Typeset by Hewer Text Composition Services, Edinburgh
Printed in Great Britain by Clays Ltd, St Ives plc

For My Mother
Elizabeth Glenconner

# Prefatory note

*Pride and Prejudice* is the most popular of Jane Austen's novels and Elizabeth Bennet was Jane Austen's favourite heroine.

As with all her novels, *Pride and Prejudice* ends in marriage: of the five daughters Mr and Mrs Bennet must marry off, three are wed, in order of precedence, as Mrs Bennet would have it, as follows: Elizabeth, the second daughter, to Mr Darcy, master of Pemberley House in Derbyshire and ten thousand a year; Jane, the eldest, to Mr Bingley, with five or six thousand a year; and Lydia, who elopes with the charming but feckless Mr Wickham. (Kitty and Mary, respectively empty-headed and bookish, remain at the end of the book in need of a husband.)

That Jane Austen continued to think of her characters after the book closed is shown in a letter – amongst many in which she used to joke about the personalities of Jane and Elizabeth Bennet – to her sister, from London in May 1813. Here she pretends she has been searching for likenesses of the Bennet sisters in the art exhibitions of the time. "Henry and I went to the exhibition in Spring Gardens," she wrote. "I was very well pleased . . . with a small portrait of Mrs Bingley, excessively like her . . . She is dressed in a white gown, with green ornaments, which convinces me of what I had always supposed, that green was a favourite colour with her. I dare say Mrs D. will be in yellow." But she records later that she was disappointed in her quest. At an exhibition of Sir Joshua Reynolds's paintings, "there was nothing like Mrs D. . . . I can only imagine that Mr D. prizes any picture of her too much to like it should be exposed to the public eye. I can imagine he would have that sort of feeling – that mixture of love, pride and delicacy." Jane Austen's characters lived on in her mind long after they had married and were, supposedly, living happily ever after.

*Pemberley* starts after the marriage of Elizabeth to Mr Darcy, and Jane to Mr Bingley. Elizabeth lives with her husband at Pemberley; and Jane and her husband have bought in a neighbouring county – which is to say, Yorkshire.

Mrs Bennet, recently widowed, has left her home, Longbourn, in Hertfordshire, but has not moved far: she is in a smaller house near Meryton, the local town she has visited with her daughters over the past quarter of a century.

Lady Catherine de Bourgh lives still at Rosings with her unmarried daughter.

Lydia, the youngest Bennet daughter to marry, leads a rootless existence with her husband and family: the Wickhams are frequently in debt, and known to sponge off Lydia's richer sisters.

# Part One

# One

It is a truth universally acknowledged, that a married man in possession of a good fortune must be in want of a son and heir.

So at least are the sentiments of all those related on both sides of the family; and there are others, besides, who might do better to keep their tongues from wagging on the fecundity or otherwise of a match.

"My dear Mrs Bennet," said Mrs Long one day to her friend, who was newly removed from Longbourn since the death of her husband, "do not you have a happy event to look forward to? I expect daily to hear news of your daughter Elizabeth and the charming Mr Darcy. I am most surprised to have heard nothing yet."

Mrs Bennet replied that she was not accustomed to hear from her daughter every day of the week.

"The news of an impending arrival in the family need only be communicated once," said Mrs Long. "Unless," she added after some reflection, "a girl is born first, and then there will need to be further communications, to be sure."

"My dear Mrs Long," said Mrs Bennet, who was accustomed to these taunts but was still unable to bear them, "I have enough to do, settling into this small house with only Mary to keep me company; and *she* is always in the library, as poor Mr Bennet was, when we were at Longbourn. I have no time for such speculations."

"You show all the courage in the world," replied Mrs Long; "and this is well known at Meryton. To have your home taken from you when you have many years to live yet . . ."

"And two daughters still unmarried," said Mrs Bennet, glad

to find herself in a conversation more agreeable to her. "For even if Kitty does stay with my dear Jane at Barlow, and with Lizzy at Pemberley, the girl is unmarried and may return here any day now, to eat me out of house and home."

Mrs Long remarked that the entail of Longbourn to a distant male cousin, Mr Collins, had been a great misfortune to the Bennet family; and she remarked again that Mrs Bennet's fortitude and bravery in removing from her home was noted by the whole neighbourhood.

"I am very well provided for here," said Mrs Bennet, who did not care for the excessive sympathy of the neighbourhood. "Mr Darcy has been most generous, as you know, and has enabled me to buy this house. Mr Bennet, I am sorry to say, made no provision for his wife and daughters."

"To have Mr Darcy as a son-in-law must be wonderful indeed," said Mrs Long. "You must feel truly indebted to him, for none of us can see that you would have had a roof over your head if your Elizabeth had not married a man with a generous nature and ten thousand a year."

"On the contrary," cried Mrs Bennet, who again disliked the way in which Mrs Long turned the conversation, "it is Mr Darcy who must be indebted to me."

"And why is that?"

"I am the mother of Elizabeth. She could not have come into the world without me."

"True indeed," said Mrs Long, who had seen out of the window that a letter had been brought into the house by the groom and was carried in to Mrs Bennet by the maid. "Without you, Mrs Bennet" – and here Mrs Long waited, as Mrs Bennet was obliged to open the letter in her presence – "without you I believe there must never be an heir to Pemberley at all."

There was silence as Mrs Bennet read the letter and then tucked it away in her writing-box.

"I hope the letter contains news that you have been hoping for," said Mrs Long when Mrs Bennet offered no information.

"Indeed it does," said Mrs Bennet, who went to the door and called up the stairs for Mary.

4

"I am glad of that," said Mrs Long, who showed no intention of moving from her chair.

Mrs Bennet brought Mary into the room and took her book from her hand as she did so. "Mary, we are invited to Pemberley for Christmas. You must have some new clothes. We shall go into Meryton. I shall order the carriage."

"I am so very glad your mother and yourself are invited to Pemberley at last," cried Mrs Long. "I hear it is a splendid house, with beautiful woods, and ten miles' walk to go round the park."

"I would rather stay here," said Mary. "My cousin Mr Collins at Longbourn has a new theological treatise for us to discuss when I next go there."

Mrs Bennet came back into the room and soon the three ladies found themselves in the hall and preparing to go to Meryton.

"Mark my words," said Mrs Long to Mrs Bennet once they were all three embarked on an expedition to dressmaker and milliner, "you are asked there, as befits your rank as the mother of Mrs Fitzwilliam Darcy, in order that you shall hear some very important news."

"And what might that be?" cried Mrs Bennet in exasperation.

# Two

Elizabeth Bennet and Mr Darcy had been married nearly a year when the invitation came for Mrs Bennet and Elizabeth's younger sister Mary to spend Christmas at Pemberley House.

The reason for the delay in inviting her mother and sister lay with Elizabeth: she had much to learn, or so she argued to herself, when it came to being mistress of Pemberley; and obligations to estate workers and tenants, as well as the setting up of a model dairy and the reconstruction of a fruit and kitchen garden long neglected, had left her little time to consider her family.

She had, of course, been much grieved by the death of her father, and with Mr Darcy had attended the funeral and stayed at Longbourn while legalities due on the making of the entail to Mr Collins were completed. She had thanked her husband wholeheartedly for his kindness and generosity in buying Meryton Lodge, on the outskirts of the little town, for her mother and two unmarried sisters. But she disliked, if the truth were to be told, to be beholden to anyone, especially Mr Darcy, for he had already given her so much that she was embarrassed to thank him further. Just as Mrs Bennet had predicted, Eliza received jewels and fine horses and carriages in far greater abundance than her sister Jane Bingley, who lived in wedded bliss with Mr Bingley at Barlow, not thirty miles away. There was nothing Elizabeth Darcy wanted that would ever be refused to her, and this sometimes made her fear that her fortune was too great to last. Mr Darcy was generous in his love as well as in his gifts; and the more he showered on his wife, the less she felt able to ask for further kindnesses.

Elizabeth knew very well that to mention a visit from her mother would prompt Mr Darcy to ever greater feats of imaginative munificence. Mrs Bennet would be encouraged, as Kitty had been until Jane had insisted she leave Pemberley and go to the Bingleys at Barlow, to stay indefinitely as his guest. A tutor or music master would in all probability be found for Mary, to help train her voice and keep her from the boredom she would feel away from her books. Mrs Bennet would have the run of the place; and be encouraged, too, to invite those of her acquaintance who lived in the vicinity. Elizabeth feared they would be many.

These were not the only reasons for Mrs Bennet's long wait for the letter which would summon her to her daughter and son-in-law's house. Elizabeth had also begun to fear that she was not able to conceive a child. However many times her sister Jane, who was the happy mother of a daughter of one year and expected another child in the near future, told her sister Lizzy that a space of a year without conception meant nothing, Elizabeth secretly fretted and grieved over the matter. She did not hope to hear her mother on the subject; and said as much to Jane, on the occasion of a visit to Barlow.

"My dear Lizzy," said Jane when she had heard her out, "nothing will stop you from conceiving a child more than the worrying about it. And if you do not invite Mother and Mary for Christmas, your own lack of charity will make you worry all the more. You are hardly known for your meanness of spirit – remember that."

Eliza thought long on her sister's words when she returned to Pemberley. It was true, her holding back from giving her mother the pleasure and excitement she so needed after the loss of her husband had come to seem exceedingly parsimonious. She was not known for this quality. It was as if the great-heartedness and generosity of Mr Darcy had taken away any spirit of giving in herself – or so she reflected. And it occurred to her that Mr Darcy himself might also consider Elizabeth's failure to invite her closest relatives less than he had expected in the warm and open nature for which, as he had so often lovingly said, he had married her. Had she become close and ungiving since she had entered the paradise that marriage to Mr Darcy and the beauties of Pemberley so undoubtedly were? The thought made her colour up, even when alone; and a tap on the door followed by a visit from Mrs Reynolds the housekeeper, with a request as to foodstuffs and game to be prepared for Christmas, finally jolted her into going downstairs to find Mr Darcy before giving any orders for kitchen or larder.

Mr Darcy, as she had known he would be, was geniality itself. Of course Mrs Bennet should come – and stay as long as she pleased. Mary should have the run of the library, which was second to none in the country. Kitty should come, to make up the party: it was a long time since she had been reunited with her mother and sister.

Elizabeth went into Mr Darcy's arms and nearly wept at the ease with which all this had been accomplished. She did not feel an obligation to Mr Darcy – rather that he had looked forward to her request, and had been too delicate to mention the matter of her mother's visit by himself. Both husband and wife were smiling and close together when Georgiana Darcy came into the room and stopped, seeing them there.

Elizabeth was overjoyed to see her sister-in-law and came to meet her in the long gallery with words of welcome. Friendship with Georgiana was the one way, so Elizabeth felt, in which she could repay Mr Darcy for his good heart and kindness to her. The girl, older than Elizabeth's sister Mary, and taller than Elizabeth herself, had nevertheless been nervous at her brother's marriage and difficult to coax out of her shell. She had spent all her childhood at Pemberley; and Elizabeth's first task was to tell her that she should spend all the time there that she wished. Georgiana, who had suffered the intolerable humiliation of a near-abduction by a fortune-hunter when she had been only fifteen years old, was also shy at her prospects of finding anyone to marry. Her aunt Lady Catherine de Bourgh had frightened her with parties and balls at Rosings, which had produced nothing but a dread in the girl of meeting anyone socially.

Elizabeth took Georgiana's arm and led her over to

Mr Darcy. She told her gently that there would be a family party at Pemberley at Christmas; and that Mary looked forward to meeting Lizzy's new sister. Mr Darcy beamed; Mrs Reynolds was given her orders; and Elizabeth wondered why she had delayed for so long in issuing this simple invitation.

# Three

Mrs Bennet lost no time informing her acquaintances of her important news. She went first to Meryton, to call on Lady Lucas; and issued a list of orders to her daughter Mary as she went out of the door.

"You are just like your father, Mary, always in the library! Are you aware of how many days remain before we leave for Pemberley? Your dresses are creased; you should pack the yellow and the blue, but the red does not become you at all!

"There will be a large staff at Pemberley, I have no doubt; but it is better to arrive with a dress that is creased, yet shows sign of having seen the iron, than a merely creased one.

"Pack your music, Mary. In such an establishment as Pemberley there may well be a music master or something of the kind in residence. The assembled company will wish to hear you sing.

"Make sure to pack your paints. I have heard that Miss Georgiana Darcy is extremely proficient with her sketches and water-colours, and you may visit Matlock, if not the Peaks!

"Hurry, Mary, there is so much to do here before we leave!"

As none of these injunctions and instructions received any reply, Mrs Bennet hastened to Meryton to receive the compliments that must be due to her. She was disturbed, therefore, to find Lady Lucas a great deal more caught up in her own affairs than receptive to Mrs Bennet's.

"Dear Mrs Bennet, you must forgive me! But I have heard such momentous news just this minute that I hardly know whether I am on my head or my heels!" cried Lady Lucas once Mrs Bennet had taken her place in a chair by the fire.

Mrs Bennet was disagreeably surprised; but tried to conceal it. "It is not a matter concerning the health of your dear husband, I trust? I find since the sad loss of Mr Bennet that wives turn to widows under my very eyes; if there has been one there have been ten husbands taken ill suddenly in the past year. I have found it hard to call anywhere."

"No, no, indeed." Lady Lucas was smiling, excessively in the opinion of Mrs Bennet. "It could be said to affect the health, certainly. But in a way that is joyful in the extreme."

If Mrs Bennet suspected the truth of Lady Lucas's happy tidings, she gave no sign of it.

"I came to tell you of my plans," she said stiffly. "They are also the plans of my dear Mary; and I anticipated that you would be glad for us."

"I'm sure I shall be," cried Lady Lucas, coming over and taking her friend's hand. "Clearly, we all have reason to rejoice today. But you must be the first to know – there are many reasons for you to be the first to rejoice with us. In short," said Lady Lucas, biting her lip at the embarrassment that was to follow and which in her excitement she had not fully accounted for, "my dear Charlotte has told us today that she expects a child in the summer!"

Mrs Bennet's stillness, for a woman known for constant and frequently agitated movement, was remarkable. Finally, she inclined her head and gave her compliments. "You must understand, my dear Lady Lucas, that this has come as a considerable shock to me. I reared five daughters at Longbourn. We spent twenty-three of the happiest years in the house. I married three of my daughters – two most advantageously, I may say – from Longbourn House. Then . . ." – and here Mrs Bennet's lip quivered and she brushed a tear from her eye – "then Mr Bennet died and I was thrown out, *evicted* with my two unmarried daughters."

Lady Lucas replied calmly that the facts of the male entail on Longbourn had been known to all of them for the duration of those years.

"A distant cousin, Mr Collins!" cried Mrs Bennet, as if this were news and not the other. "Mr Collins inherits Longbourn

11

and is in there before poor dear Mr Bennet is cold in his grave!"

"Mrs Bennet!" said Lady Lucas. But her pleading was to no avail.

"I know that this is not the fault of your daughter Charlotte," said Mrs Bennet magnanimously. "My Lizzy refused Mr Collins's proposal of marriage and dear Charlotte was lucky indeed to find a husband."

"Thank you for your compliments," replied Lady Lucas coldly. "The strong possibility of Charlotte's pregnancy has perhaps made us late in extending an invitation to you to visit Longbourn."

"And what if Charlotte has nothing but daughters!" cried Mrs Bennet, whose thoughts had run far ahead of her. "Then she will know the mortification of expulsion from her home when still in the prime of life!"

The maid came in with tea at this point, which made a welcome interruption. Mrs Bennet had to wipe the tears from her eyes, and arrange her face to give an impression of extreme joy at the prospects of an heir to Longbourn.

"We all wish to invite you to Longbourn for Christmas," said Lady Lucas when the maid had gone. "And Mary must come too. Even if there are painful memories, there will also be joyful ones. Charlotte is to write to you today; but her news, as I say, has made her late in extending the invitation."

Mrs Bennet set down her cup the better to enjoy her advantage. "I must decline your and Mrs Collins's kind invitation," she said slowly and clearly.

"Mrs Bennet – do reconsider!" cried Lady Lucas, who was much disturbed by the strange manner of her friend.

"We go to Pemberley," Mrs Bennet said after a long pause during which the tea things were cleared and the maid went out again. "So it is with great regret that Mary and I will be unable to accept."

"Goodness," said Lady Lucas warmly, for she wished to make amends to Mrs Bennet and saw how deeply she had offended her. "This is momentous news indeed! You will stay with Elizabeth and Mr Darcy," she added, though there was no necessity for her to do so.

"I am accustomed to having my family round me at Christmas," Mrs Bennet said. "Pemberley will be on a grander scale than Longbourn I don't doubt; but the company is what matters, don't you agree?"

"I do," said Lady Lucas, eager not to show her relief at the prospect of a quiet Christmas with her daughter. "So who will be assembled at Pemberley when you go?"

"I have written to my daughter Jane Bingley," Mrs Bennet replied in a lofty tone, "telling her I expect her to be at Pemberley at Christmas. With all her family, it goes without saying. Mr Bingley has bought a fine estate at Barlow; but I should find it sadly inconvenient to go between one daughter and another. Jane expects a child in the New Year and she will be more comfortable at Pemberley."

"You did not tell me that Jane expected another child so soon!" cried Lady Lucas, who now felt thoroughly uncomfortable at her lack of delicacy in her conversation with Mrs Bennet. "I am too caught up in dear Charlotte, I expect."

"It is not of great consequence," said Mrs Bennet coldly. She rose to take her leave and Lady Lucas accompanied her into the hall.

"I was on my way to Longbourn," Mrs Bennet said, "to offer the compliments of the season to dear Charlotte, as I shall sadly not be able to invite you all over to Meryton Lodge for an evening, as I had anticipated."

Lady Lucas, glad to see the breach mended, said she would accompany Mrs Bennet to Longbourn, and they walked down the lane together.

# Four

Mrs Bennet was warmly received in the house that had been her home for close on a quarter of a century; and after she had expressed surprise and concern at the furnishings installed by the new owners she allowed herself to be led into the sitting-room and seated in her favourite chair.

Charlotte, daughter of Lady Lucas and wife of Mr Collins, was in a high flutter to find the mother of her great friend Elizabeth Bennet on her first visit to Longbourn since the death of Mr Bennet; and her chief concern, after receiving compliments on the child to be born the following year, was to hear of her friend's health and well-being.

"Lizzy is very well," said Mrs Bennet. "She has her hands full at present, so she assures me, with a new kitchen garden and a model dairy, not to mention plans for further enlarging the stream in the park into a semblance of moving water staircases. Or that is how she wrote it to me," Mrs Bennet added doubtfully.

"Ah, so she is well occupied indeed," cried Mr Collins, who had seated his mother-in-law Lady Lucas on the far side of the fire and sat in a devout and conjugal pose with Charlotte on a sofa. "I hope Mrs Darcy has also the welfare of the men and their wives and children at Pemberley under consideration. According to Mr Darcy's aunt Lady Catherine de Bourgh," Mr Collins went on before Mrs Bennet could find the opportunity to emphasise the care given to the workers at Pemberley by her daughter, "Mr Darcy has always shown extraordinary kindness to the poor."

"I am sure Elizabeth will not deflect him from this," said Mrs Bennet.

14

"My dear lady, please do not imagine that I imply anything other than the most meticulous attentions to the villagers on the part of Mrs Darcy. It is simply a matter of upbringing: Elizabeth has not grown up in such a station as Mr Darcy's and the scale of bounty which Mr Darcy's dear mother Lady Anne was accustomed to distribute may be unfamiliar to her."

Silence greeted this, and Lady Lucas asked Mrs Bennet where her youngest married daughter Lydia would be spending Christmas.

"Ah, I am glad to hear of dear Lydia," cried Mr Collins. "She is well, I hope?"

Mrs Bennet said her daughter Lydia was certainly well.

"Whenever I hear of another birth in the Wickham family I feel the loss of my position as parson at Hunsford," Mr Collins exclaimed. "I used to find the baptism of infants the most rewarding aspect of my calling. To take a pagan soul – to bring the first touch of God to a child – why, it is a most affecting thing!" As Mrs Bennet nodded coldly, Mr Collins pressed his point. "Mr and Mrs Wickham must have a growing number of children by now, Mrs Bennet. How many are there?"

Mrs Bennet replied that her youngest daughter and her husband had four children under four years old.

"They are blessed indeed!" said Lady Lucas quietly, for she wished to arrest Mr Collins in his path.

"You have a quantity of grandchildren then," cried Mr Collins, "for Mr and Mrs Bingley also have brought forth, have they not?"

Mrs Bennet said that her daughter Jane expected a second child in the New Year.

"Six grandchildren!" said Charlotte with a sweet smile, for her own condition prevented her from seeing the annoyance in Mrs Bennet's face. "How fortunate you are!"

As Mrs Bennet agreed to this, Mr Collins pressed home. "I dare say you await the birth of one more, to bring your cup to overflowing," he said in a tone that caused even Lady Lucas, grateful as she was to have her daughter settled at Longbourn,

15

to rise and remark it was growing dark already and they must be on their way back to Meryton.

"The days are so short," Mrs Bennet agreed, rising from her chair also.

"Please, do not leave before we extend an invitation to you," said Mr Collins, taking Mrs Bennet's hand and bowing deeply. "Both I and Charlotte have thought deeply of your position, alone and grieving, over Christmas at Meryton. We extend to you with the utmost cordiality an invitation to spend those days here at Longbourn."

"I go to Pemberley for Christmas," said Mrs Bennet.

"Some of your memories, on returning to your old home, may be painful," said Mr Collins, who had not heard this. "But others will surely be joyful. Charity begins at home." He laughed in an awkward way. "And in what was your home and is now ours we wish to invite you – "

"Sir William awaits me," said Lady Lucas hastily. "Will you come and dine with us?" she asked Mrs Bennet as she steered her friend to the door.

"I have too much to do, preparing for my journey to Pemberley," replied Mrs Bennet.

Mr Collins stared at her in amazement. "You go to Pemberley for Christmas? My dear Mrs Bennet, you will find yourself in the most exalted company. Lady Catherine de Bourgh communicated to me only yesterday in a letter that she will go to Pemberley for Christmas."

Mrs Bennet stopped by the door.

"I believe you had the honour of receiving Lady Catherine here at Longbourn," said Mr Collins.

Mrs Bennet kept silent, recalling Lady Catherine's visit and her pronouncement on the very sitting-room in which they were all now assembled: that "this must be a most inconvenient sitting-room for the evening, in summer; the windows are full west." Mrs Bennet also heard her own reassurances to Lady Catherine that they never sat there after dinner; and her own reply to her visitor's remark that the park at Longbourn was very small: "I assure you it is much larger than Sir William Lucas's"; and to cover her embarrassment

16

asked Charlotte if she would come over to Meryton Lodge before she and Mary left for Pemberley.

"Charlotte has too much to do, preparing for our Nativity pageant," Mr Collins said before his wife could reply. "It will not be on the scale of the festivities at Pemberley, I am sure, but we are satisfied with it."

After further allusions to the nativity of both God and the expected junior Collins, Mrs Bennet was able to take her leave.

"You will tell Lizzy I miss her ever so much," cried poor Charlotte as Mrs Bennet put on her shawl in the hall, "and give my fondest regards to dear Jane also."

"You will be reunited with all your daughters save Lydia," said Mr Collins. "But it costs far too dear to transport a family of such a size around England. I should not impart this to you, but I must . . ." And here Mr Collins stepped in front of his mother-in-law and spoke close to Mrs Bennet's ear. "It will come best from you, Madam, if you inform dear Lydia that we are not rich, here."

"What do you mean?" cried Mrs Bennet, alarmed.

"Mrs Wickham approaches us for money," said Mr Collins. "The estate left by Mr Bennet – excuse me – gives no more than two thousand a year. Your own portion, Madam, you took with you."

"I should think so," replied Mrs Bennet, drawing herself up.

"Charlotte has a kind heart. But she cannot take from the housekeeping and give to your daughter, Mrs Bennet. I pride myself on noticing the table we keep. We cannot lower our standard of living here at Longbourn in order to subsidise Mr and Mrs Wickham and their family."

"No, indeed," said Mrs Bennet, who was too taken aback to say anything.

"I wrote and directed Lydia to her sister Mrs Darcy," said Mr Collins. "I do believe the housekeeping at Pemberley would hardly show the difference."

# Five

Elizabeth received the news at Pemberley that Mrs Bennet had begged Jane and her family to join them for Christmas with extreme despondency. She loved Jane; Mr Bingley remained a very good friend of Mr Darcy; but the thought of bringing another household for which she felt herself almost entirely responsible under the roof at Pemberley threatened her with a repetition of those Christmases at Longbourn before the sisters had married and gone north. Mrs Bennet would talk at her daughters without cease; Kitty and Mary would be urged to find young men, which would alarm and annoy Mr Darcy, so Elizabeth could imagine, and the harmony of their days at Pemberley would be badly disrupted.

Perhaps also because Mr and Mrs Bennet had had so unsatisfactory a marriage, Elizabeth had no desire to re-create the family circle in a house which she admired but did not yet feel completely at home in. Mr Bennet's contempt for his wife, and sad neglect of all her sisters, if not herself, might make itself felt at Pemberley. Mr Darcy, whom she had set out to soften, was certainly more approachable, less harsh, and a good deal less proud than he had shown himself before they wed. But a protracted stay from Mrs Bennet, not to speak of the chattering Kitty and the intensity of Mary, might return him to those ways before they were banished for ever. To add Jane and Mr Bingley and their ménage would surely surround him too completely with her family.

There was another reason why Elizabeth was loath to mention the contents of Jane's letter to her husband. The Bingleys might have Mr Bingley's sister staying with them at Barlow; and she would most certainly be included in the

18

invitation, if it was forthcoming. Miss Bingley, as Elizabeth knew too well, had had designs on Mr Darcy, and had spoken very ill of Miss Bennet, in her determination to be mistress of Pemberley. Her presence would hardly be a soothing one; and her jokes at the expense of Mrs Bennet were audible to Elizabeth before they were even uttered. However, if the subject was not brought up by Elizabeth to Mr Darcy today, her mother would bring it up on arrival; and there would be consternation and disappointment at her daughter's refusal to bring all the family together at the time of Mrs Bennet's first Christmas since her bereavement.

Mr Darcy was walking across the bridge in front of the house when Elizabeth, seeing him from a window, ran out to meet him.

Even after nearly a year of marriage, she was surprised each time she saw Mr Darcy at the flutter it set up in her. He was handsome, certainly; but there was something in him which was more than that: a gravity which lightened only in a delightful way when he saw her; a presence which, however often she told herself was hers for all her life, seemed remote, mysterious and ever-alluring to her.

Elizabeth found she was living happily ever after, as in the old fairy-tales; and there was not enough she could do to show Darcy her appreciation of it. How fortunate, then, that her shy declaration of the contents of her sister Jane's letter brought a smile to Darcy's lips, and an avowal that he too had something he was in need of telling her.

"You make me happy with your request, sweetest, loveliest Eliza," said Mr Darcy, twinkling down at her as if the thought of a whole basket of Bennets came as nothing but a pleasant surprise to him. "I am happy to see Jane; I shall have a good few games of backgammon with Bingley; and, as for Miss Bingley, I think she cannot hold a candle to you, Lizzy."

Elizabeth owned quietly to the fact that she found the size of Pemberley daunting still; that a large party could move in there without the inconvenience this would have caused at Longbourn was still incredible to her.

"You are the mistress of Pemberley, Elizabeth," said

Mr Darcy and, despite the park being a place where the public could, and did, walk, and despite the eyes of servants from the wide wall of windows in the house, he took her in his arms and kissed her tenderly. "You shall invite whomsoever you please," he said.

The couple walked on, and down into the grotto, where the berries on the holly led Mr Darcy to remark that some should be brought into the house before Christmas.

"And now I must confess to you," he said, "for I too have received a letter. Lady Catherine de Bourgh, my aunt, was always accustomed to come to Pemberley for Christmas, with her daughter. You remember Lady Catherine, I have no doubt?"

"I do," said Elizabeth, but she repressed a shudder for the sake of Mr Darcy. The insolence Lady Catherine had shown her in the past should certainly never be repeated; and she had Darcy to protect her, now she was married.

"I am happy to welcome Lady Catherine and her daughter to Pemberley," said Elizabeth, and she banished thoughts of Mrs Bennet and Darcy's aunt together as quickly as they came to her.

Darcy and his wife crossed the stream again at its lowest point, in the water garden, and were met by the head gardener, with whom they engaged in a lively conversation as to the feasibility of training water to descend a part of the park in cascades.

"I like the idea," said Mr Darcy, who was in high good humour. "And we shall plant some young trees down there, where the deer can't get at them!"

Elizabeth took Darcy's arm and they strolled up through the park to the house. Whether the mention of young trees or the sight of windows of the unused west wing set her thoughts in train she would not afterwards be able to say; but Elizabeth now was to know a sense of stinging mortification never once suffered in all the time of her marriage to Mr Darcy. She remarked on the happy time Jane's little daughter would have at Pemberley. "We could open up the old nurseries," she said, pointing to the windows and clasping Darcy's arm closer to her side.

But Mr Darcy broke loose of her grasp and strode up the hill in silence. For all the rest of the day, however much Elizabeth tried to extract the reason for his displeasure from him, he was as dark and quiet and proud as he had been when she first met him as a guest of Mr Bingley at Netherfield. Elizabeth was left to wonder at her own presumption in telling the master of Pemberley how the bedchambers should be allocated, and she spent the rest of the day in a solitary roaming of the house, for, as she owned to herself, there were rooms and landings she had never even entered.

It was in one of these, on a dark landing, where she stood fixed by the gaze of a Darcy ancestor in a long portrait on the wall, that Elizabeth felt a slight touch on her shoulder and turned to find the features of Mr Darcy smiling down at her.

"My dearest Eliza," Mr Darcy said, "you shall open up any part of the house. For it is all yours now, as you know, and my heart along with it."

Elizabeth wept with relief as she went into his arms. Yet she knew that she must go carefully when it came to the ordering of Pemberley, and she resolved to keep the Christmas house party strictly to the timetable and the numbers agreed.

This, alas, was not to prove as easy as she had hoped.

# Six

Jane Bingley was as much distressed by Mrs Bennet's letter as was her sister Elizabeth, on receipt of the intelligence that their mother found nothing wrong in dictating her daughters' movements to them. A long day walking in the park of the house the Bingleys had bought at Barlow was needed for the sisters to assure each other of an enduring love and esteem; and for Jane to feel able to accept the invitation to Pemberley which Elizabeth pressed on her. And Elizabeth needed to know that Jane did not accept merely to alleviate the worst effects of Mrs Bennet. It was hard for her to tell the truth – to so charming, easy-going and complaisant a character as Jane, at least – that she did not yet feel fully mistress of Pemberley and that this was the reason for the absence of an invitation to the Bingleys, over the festive season. Only Jane, as Elizabeth acknowledged when her sister threw her arms round her neck and said she knew all this without the telling, could be counted on to understand and condone any action, however apparently heartless. Elizabeth had often in the past feared this trait in Jane: that she believed no bad of any living being, only good; now she was to be profoundly grateful for it. Her understanding of Jane's tolerance was to be tried to the extreme, however, when on her next visit to Barlow Jane produced another letter, just arrived.

"I can scarcely believe it," said Jane as she handed the letter to her sister. "Lydia comes north and takes a house at Rowsley. She pretends she will stay with aunt Gardiner, 'if there are no houses to be taken'. Oh, Lizzy, could Mama have put her up to this?"

As Elizabeth read and re-read the letter, Emily Bingley,

Jane's small daughter, ran in and out; and, for all the horror of receiving Lydia's latest missive, Elizabeth was unable to refrain from smiling at the child, and showing the rise in spirits which Emily's presence inevitably brought about. It was one reason, though Elizabeth hardly acknowledged it to herself, for her frequent visits to Barlow (and one more reason for inviting her dear sister and her husband for Christmas): this perpetual, pattering delight in the rooms of the house her sister and Mr Bingley had found as a place to raise their family; a reason to come again and again, always expecting and receiving the sweet smiles and simple love of the child.

Elizabeth knew that Pemberley would be transformed one day, as her sister Jane and Mr Bingley's home had been, by the presence of children. But now it was dark and forbidding to her, a house that had been a bachelor's house too long, where even a loving wife – and an efficient housekeeper – could not keep at bay the sense of the end of a cycle, of the supremacy of the ghosts of the past over the living. The coming of little Emily Bingley to Pemberley at Christmas might be a painful reminder, to Elizabeth, of her own failure, so far, to become a mother; but a part of her thought, too, that the presence of her niece could encourage the conceiving of a child for herself and Darcy at Pemberley.

For the time, however, less welcome small Wickhams were due to appear any day; and Elizabeth found, as often before, that her assumptions and prejudices were kindly and gently rebutted by her sister Jane.

"She simply wishes to come to Pemberley!" cried Elizabeth. "Lydia knows full well that aunt Gardiner has had no house at Rowsley for ten years at least. Why, when I journeyed north with aunt and uncle Gardiner" – and here Elizabeth knew she blushed, for she recalled so clearly her first visit to Pemberley as a tourist, when it was thought the family was away; and how Mr Darcy had rounded a box hedge in the garden and how delightfully surprised they both had been, after the first embarrassment – "even then," Elizabeth continued, "we put up at lodgings. Lydia knows she has no aunt Gardiner to visit. And she knows Rowsley is but five miles from Pemberley. Why did she not write to me directly, if she wishes to come as a guest to the house?"

"It could be that she thought you would refuse her," said the simple, good-hearted Jane, "with Mr Wickham so much disliked by Mr Darcy, ever since he was a young man."

"She writes to you because she believes you will find a way to persuade me," cried Elizabeth. "It isn't fair on you, Jane; for I shall never be persuaded."

Mr Bingley came into the room at this point and remarked that he had heard a forceful tone and had come to see if assistance was in order. This was said with a twinkle, for Mr Bingley was as good-natured as his wife. It was nevertheless awkward for Elizabeth to have to give the reason for her raised voice – which had in fact frightened little Emily and sent her scampering from the room.

"Lizzy has read Lydia's letter," said Jane by way of explanation.

"I believe our mother has done all this!" cried Elizabeth, who did not want her refusal of her younger sister as a guest at Pemberley to be relayed in too blunt a manner to Mr Bingley. "It can only come from her: it's some notion of getting us all together."

"I would not be sorry of that," said Jane in as quiet a tone as Elizabeth's had been feverish. "But you are the mistress of Pemberley, Lizzy, and you are to have the final word. Poor Lydia," she added, as Elizabeth looked about for a way of escape and saw none. "She will find lodgings at Rowsley if she does not leave it too late, I am sure."

"I know a farmer who lets rooms just by here," said Mr Bingley. "Emily will like to go from Pemberley and play with her Wickham cousins when we are all there at Christmas."

"I will talk to Darcy," said Elizabeth, for she saw with bitterness that Lydia and Mr Wickham could hardly be seen to be excluded from so large a house at a time of pious rejoicing. "I do not think Mr Darcy will want Mr Wickham in the house," was all she had to fall back on, now.

"A man as violently in love with his wife as Darcy is with you, my dear Eliza, would not care if there were a dozen Mr Wickhams in the house," said Bingley.

# Seven

The next hours passed happily enough, with little Emily made to laugh and play again by her mother and her aunt Lizzy; and Mr Bingley making a treasure-hunt in the garden that had as its final prize a doll's house constructed by Mr Bingley himself in the barn.

"It is beautifully done!" cried Elizabeth. "A handsome house indeed" – and, lifting Emily high to the windows of the bedchambers: "Look, Emily! You shall have some dolls to lie in those magnificent fourposters. And some very smart footmen to serve in the dining-room – I shall make them myself!"

Elizabeth saw the joy in her sister's eyes at the love and practicality that had gone into the making of the doll's house. She was fortunate – but here Elizabeth caught herself up and wondered at the unspoken disloyalty to her own position – her own husband, even. It was true, certainly, that Jane's husband was an easier man to be with than Elizabeth's: Mr Bingley was as sunny as a cloudless day, all geniality and smiles; whereas Mr Darcy, as Elizabeth so well knew after close on a year of marriage to him, could as little evade the dark, thunderous looks that sometimes crossed his face and lingered there as he could sidestep his position as master of Pemberley. He had so many people looking to him for comfort and support; so many decisions to be made in the course of every day that could change the future of the estate and those who worked there – those must be the reasons, Elizabeth always supposed, that he would grow so silent and aloof at times. And – and here Elizabeth sighed, set little Emily down on the floor of the barn and went to take her sister's arm, to suggest a stroll on the

26

lawns – there was no child as yet to raise Mr Darcy's spirits, no reason for him to occupy himself with childish things, as Mr Bingley so gladly did.

If it was hard to think of Mr Darcy as a being capable of so great a change in character and outlook as this (for to see him busy with the construction of a doll's house was far beyond Elizabeth's imagining) it was important to remember that such great changes did not infrequently take place when a man became a father. Mr Darcy would dote – surely he would. Yet a slender doubt remained, and Elizabeth had no wish to own it. She could not recall that Darcy had shown interest in any of the children of the estate workers; and, this being an area of chief concern to her, she had sometimes lightly wondered why this should be. Mr Darcy was kindness and generosity itself, and there was no surprise in this, when it came to hearing his Eliza's requests for funds, clothing and schooling for the children of the men who worked his land for him. All Derbyshire knew of the progressive measures the new Mrs Darcy was putting in place, and that Mr Darcy's good heart was regulated now by the practical suggestions of a wife who would steer him in the right direction. All the same, Elizabeth sensed a distance – which, again, she must put down to the great distance between these families and Mr Darcy's: they depended on him so entirely, after all – as the cause of his almost absent-minded and distracted air when the subject was broached.

"My dearest Lizzy," said Jane, for she had a gift of knowing sometimes to the point of the uncanny what transpired in her sister's mind, "are you quite certain that we will not be an imposition at Pemberley for Christmas? It is perfectly easy for us, you know, to come in the chaise for a day and put up with friends for the night before we return home. Mama would still see as much of us as she pleased, for she can come here with us when we return. She exaggerates the inconvenience of the journey greatly."

"Jane!" cried Elizabeth in return, and laughed aloud to find her fears so neatly caught once again, though she intended never to confide Mr Darcy's black mood at the mention of

27

the opening of the nurseries to her sister if she could help it. "I am such a novice at this kind of thing, that's all. I have the best housekeeper in the world – Mrs Reynolds – but I am still shy with her and I think she will discover all the little habits we had of dining and arranging ourselves at Longbourn, which would not do at Pemberley at all! No, I confess I fear the very idea of Mama and Lady Catherine de Bourgh both under one roof – and that roof mine!"

Elizabeth broke off and Jane clasped her close. "I understand, Lizzy. And my heart aches for you now that Lydia announces her intentions." She paused, then said on a quieter note: "Suppose Mr Darcy finds Lydia's children very bothersome, my dear. He is not used to them, you know. He has lived at Pemberley a bachelor so long – and Georgiana was often at Rosings with her aunt, so I've heard. Why should we then impose our own child . . .?"

"But Jane! Emily will bring the joy of Christmas to the place!" cried Elizabeth. Then, no longer able to resist, she held Jane close and murmured that she hoped the presence of the child would make it possible for her to conceive; would lift what she now began to see as a curse of childlessness that hung over Pemberley. "I do not even know any longer that Darcy wants a child as I do," she ended on so dejected a note that it was Jane's turn to laugh and tease her sister for an attack of over-sensitivity.

"Darcy is in love, Lizzy!" said Jane when they had both wiped the tears from her eyes. "It is not a sentiment of which he has much knowledge. He was accustomed always to have exactly what he pleased – as you know – for he was proud and lofty and assumed you would be flattered to accept his proposal before the words were out of his mouth. He learned he must make himself worthy of you, before you would take him."

"I was pleased to accept him when I saw what a magnificent place Pemberley is," said Elizabeth; and she and Jane both laughed again.

"There, you are feeling better already! But you must understand the novelty for Mr Darcy in this whole situation.

He loves you – and he does not think of a child yet, for you are wife, child and lover to him."

"That may be," said Elizabeth; and she turned to walk back along the lawn to the barn, where Emily played entranced with the miniature house her father had built for her.

"Have you spoken of a child with Darcy?" asked Jane as she hastened to catch Elizabeth by the door of the barn.

"Goodness, no!" came the answer; and, before Elizabeth could go on, Mr Bingley had come out from the shadows at the back of the barn with a spar of wood he would cut down as a table for the doll's house.

Mr Bingley was all affability and declared himself delighted at his forthcoming visit to Pemberley. He had stayed there at this time of year before, because, as sister Lizzy knew, he had been a good friend of Mr Darcy for as long as anyone could remember. "It will be a merry and happy place this year, with Elizabeth Darcy at the foot of the table," Mr Bingley said with gallantry. He enquired as to the party for the children of the estate workers, which was by tradition in the way of taking place just two days after Christmas Day.

"I am the organiser this year," said Elizabeth, who was by now much soothed by the sympathy of Jane and the kind interest of Mr Bingley in the party, which would be held at Pemberley. "It will have a larger number of presents and parcels to give out than before," she continued. "I do not like to ask for charity – but the neighbouring families have been generous in their donations."

"And no doubt you will invite them to the New Year's Ball at Pemberley," said Mr Bingley, as the maid came down the lawn and said Mrs Darcy's chaise was at the door.

# Eight

Pemberley had never looked so beautiful as it did today: so Elizabeth was able to reflect, as she went through the park; for, entering at one of its lowest points, she was granted the opportunity to enjoy the mystery and delicacy of the woods in winter, and to appreciate the extent of land that was covered with ancient trees. After half a mile she was at the top of a considerable eminence, and here she alighted, electing to walk down to Pemberley House, situated on the opposite side of the valley and approached by a well-tended road.

She halted awhile to look over at the handsome stone building, standing well on rising ground, and backed by a ridge of high woody hills; and she smiled to see the stream in front, widened even further under her own instructions a few months past and now forming a lake that was neither artificially swollen nor falsely adorned. All in all, the new mistress of Pemberley was confirmed yet again in her first impression, when she had come as a traveller with her aunt and uncle, that she had never seen a place for which nature had done more, or where natural beauty had been so little counteracted by an awkward taste.

Elizabeth walked down towards Pemberley as the shadows lengthened and candles were lit in the house, casting a light on the stone balustrades and gravel walks of the terraces outside. She paused again, before going to the side door she was accustomed to use – for the front door, in all its carved splendour, was opened only on formal occasions – and considered the words her kind sister Jane had spoken, and with them her own foolish attitude (sometimes, at least) to her husband and to her position as his wife.

She was in no doubt that Mr Darcy hoped for an heir one day. But that he was happy with things as they were was only too evident. His sister Georgiana, Elizabeth knew by watching first consternation and then relief in her eyes when she was with the newly wedded couple, had feared at first that Elizabeth's open, sportive nature might offend her brother. Certainly, she had learnt in the months since Elizabeth and Darcy had been together at Pemberley that there are liberties permitted to a wife that a sister more than ten years junior is not accorded; and as she felt on safer and safer ground with the spirit that now took over the old house, her expression of delight grew increasingly marked. Darcy an object of open pleasantry! It was wonderful indeed, to her, to see him unbend and soften at Elizabeth's touch. Her gratitude to her sister she tried to show with as many spontaneous demonstrations of affection as she was capable – but an absence of Elizabeth at Pemberley, even if it were only for a day, returned the girl to the shy, proud ways of her past, when she had been raised by Lady Catherine de Bourgh at Rosings. Then, she had not been permitted for the space of one moment to forget her rank – and the aloofness this required of her and of her inferiors at all times. Now, for all the joy she wished to express at the sound of Elizabeth as she opened the door into the Great Hall, she lingered at the top of the staircase and waited for the call and embrace of Mrs Darcy to come first.

Mrs Fitzwilliam Darcy! Elizabeth was sometimes herself amazed to think of the respectful manner in which she was approached by the wives of the county as well as the tenants and many retainers at Pemberley. Was she too informal, too indiscreet for them? Did she glimpse sometimes a look of dismay, as she laughed and waived the more stringent of the courtesies? She did not think so; but, as she reflected once more – and paused at the foot of the wide staircase – this was another subject on which she and Darcy shared no views. Was Jane right, that a more open, shared marriage, such as hers with Mr Bingley, would banish Elizabeth's fears and lead her to greater understanding of the man she had found herself, to her own great astonishment, to love extremely? Was not the silence, as if by tacit consent, on many matters close to Elizabeth's thoughts, a part of the allure of the union these two unlikely people had formed? It was as if, by guessing and by saying nothing, the love between them grew daily stronger. Elizabeth could not see herself demanding an interview of Mr Darcy on the subject of future progeny; and just as she knew from his warm and loving smiles that she was not too open with visiting gentry – and would be as happy as he to jest about the most foolish of them when they had gone – so she could only intuit that if Mr Darcy were fretting to see her with child, she would know it and they would talk.

Elizabeth resolved to banish her fears and suspicions and to rejoice in her happiness. She would not allow even the prospect of breaking to Mr Darcy the expected arrival of Lydia and Mr Wickham, and four little Wickhams, to spoil the happy openness and independence of spirit for which she knew he really loved her. She would not permit the sensation, which she knew to be foreign to her nature, of looking for Darcy's disapproval in his every glance, on the occasion of her family's visit to Pemberley. Christmas would be a penance that way; and her fears, she knew, were groundless. For if she, Eliza Bennet, were to be cowed by the size of Pemberley and the possible inconvenience of her husband at the company of her sisters and mother, this would set a precedent that would indeed show a marked change in her personality.

Georgiana came out of the shadows and embraced Elizabeth, her normally icy reserve melting as it always did when she saw the animated beauty of Mrs Darcy.

"There is a letter for you," she said, as Mr Darcy, coming down the long gallery, cried out in mock annoyance at his wife's walking through the park when it was already so very dark and late.

Before his sister, Darcy observed the strictest manners; and Elizabeth knew well enough not to fly into his arms at such a time. But she was unable to restrain herself when she had quickly perused the letter – though she reflected that the relief and joy she felt at the contents might baffle her husband in the extreme.

"My aunt Gardiner rents at Rowsley this Christmas," cried Elizabeth. "Is that not good of her?"

"I am pleased to hear your aunt and uncle will be at Rowsley," said Mr Darcy, gravely, but with a twinkle. "I cannot see, however, why it is so good of her to do so."

"She has Lydia and the Wickhams to stay with her," said Elizabeth; then was hard put to stop the colour flare into her cheeks; for even Darcy could not guess at the dread she had known, the battles she had fought within herself when it came to telling him: that the man with whom he had spent his childhood, and who had turned out wild and undeserving of the kindness of old Mr Darcy, would be arriving with a batch of noisy children to stay under his roof.

Georgiana went to her room, and Elizabeth and Darcy were able at last to embrace and to laugh at the prolificity of the Bennet relatives at Christmas. Elizabeth was able, too, to feel that her aunt Gardiner's delicacy had dictated this move; and that five miles, which was the distance of Rowsley from the house, was a fair distance.

# Nine

Mrs Bennet was much disturbed to find herself the recipient of an unexpected call just as she packed for her journey to Derbyshire. Mary came across the hall from the library to announce that Mr Collins was visible from those windows, alighting from a carriage with a pile of boxes under his arm.

"Boxes?" cried Mrs Bennet. "We have enough in the way of boxes, I should hope, to see us up to Pemberley."

Mary replied that the boxes Mr Collins was bearing were old and dusty and looked as if they were no use for anything at all.

"Are we so poor we must pack in old boxes?" said Mrs Bennet, who was half demented by the preparations for the trip. "Say we are not at home, Mary."

Mary took some pleasure in going to the door at too slow a pace to prevent the ingress of Mr Collins. She was now the only daughter at home (Kitty, when not staying with her sister Jane and sometimes at Pemberley, was at Lyme, as she was presently, with her aunt Philips) and the necessity of going out more into company with her mother, as well as the expectations of Mrs Bennet that Mary would sit with her in the evenings – for she could not sit alone – had brought an increasingly moralising tone to her voice and a sly pleasure in discomfiting her parent that had not been remarkable in the lifetime of Mr Bennet.

"Perhaps Mr Collins brings us deed-boxes from Long-bourn," Mary observed. "Papa often said he had left boxes in the cellar there and we were not to forget them."

Mr Collins was announced at this moment and came in bowing very profusely.

34

"My dear Mrs Bennet, you must forgive my calling at such an inopportune time. I have taken on the mantle of pater-familias, and since the much-lamented death of Mr Bennet I assume the responsibilities, as the only surviving male cousin, of head of the family."

"If you are head of the family, then why do you not arrange that we receive income from the estate?" enquired Mary.

"My dear Miss Mary," cried Mr Collins, "I am come to hand over to you these deposit boxes which were inadvertently left in the cellar of Longbourn House. Mr Bennet's boxes, Madam" – and he bowed to both mother and daughter in so ridiculous a way that Mary was unable to prevent herself from bursting out laughing.

"Oh my nerves!" cried Mrs Bennet. "This is no time for legal matters, Mr Collins. Can it not wait?"

"It is entirely a matter for your discretion, Mrs Bennet," said Mr Collins, sounding very grave.

"Oh goodness – suppose they annul the entail on Longbourn," cried Mrs Bennet. "I know Mr Bennet tried with lawyers to do some justice to his poor wife and daughters. Indeed, just before he died some boxes *did* arrive in the mail from London. Oh dear, what if we are to move back into our dear home again? And if we do, how can we also go north to Pemberley for Christmas?"

The maid announced Mrs Long, who now bustled into the room as if it were she and not Mrs Bennet who was about to undertake an arduous journey to Derbyshire. She held a parcel, wrapped in brown paper. "Mrs Bennet, do please forgive me! I have taken more time over this than I intended. But it has been a labour of love, you know, and I ask no more reward than a little news of progress – from time to time, that is all I ask."

"Mrs Long, what are you talking about?" said Mary.

Mrs Bennet said her nerves were now at their worst point since the death of Mr Bennet. "Everyone brings boxes and parcels to Meryton Lodge! Are we to accomplish our journey encumbered with all this?"

"Mrs Bennet, you are far from well," said Mrs Long,

drawing herself up. "I will open the package for you, if you insist, and take my leave."

"Mrs Long, do please forgive me! And I have not even offered refreshment!" cried poor Mrs Bennet.

"I will take lemonade," said Mr Collins.

"Mary – go and tell Becca. No! Stay and open these boxes with me, for I may faint away if they contain a legal document that changes the course of my life and that of my remaining unmarried daughters!"

"And what could that be?" said Mrs Long, who placed her parcel on the window-sill and came over to the deed-boxes.

"No less than the annulment of the entail, a matter on which Mr Bennet was working most assiduously at the time of his death. Oh dear," as another thought struck her, "who will then inherit Longbourn? Why, my daughter Jane Bingley, for she is the eldest. Mr Bingley will certainly be surprised to find himself just three miles from Netherfield. He will wonder at the hand of Fate, that he should rent one house in Hertfordshire, marry the daughter of his neighbour and then inherit the daughter's house!"

"There is nothing in here," said Mary, who had come back into the room and opened the boxes. "They are empty, Mr Collins."

"But I hope a fine deed-box in good condition may be of some value," replied Mr Collins. "We are in need of the cellar at Longbourn, for we must store there the furniture from the upper room we intend as a nursery. We cannot store Mr Bennet's effects indefinitely."

Mrs Long now took the opportunity of handing her parcel to Mrs Bennet; but, seeing that the parcel remained unopened on her lap, she tore off the paper herself and held up a small garment, at which the assembled company gaped in silence.

"I have become extremely proficient at smocking," said Mrs Long when no comment was forthcoming. "This is a child's smock, Mrs Bennet."

"Why, so it is," said Mrs Bennet in a faint voice.

"The very facsimile of a young farmer's smock," said Mr Collins, bowing to Mrs Long.

36

"For your grandson, Mrs Bennet," said Mrs Long, who was unable to contain her excitement any longer.

"My daughter Jane has a daughter, Emily," said Mrs Bennet. "It is true that Jane may give birth while at Pemberley, for she is near her time. I shall warn Lizzy of this. I am sure Mr Darcy will be most understanding and that the accommodation at Pemberley will be entirely sufficient for an accouchement."

"Indeed, Mrs Bingley will bring more happiness into your life very soon, Mrs Bennet. But I mean this smock to be worn at Pemberley; and to be handed down the generations too. Make sure Nurse starches it not too much, for this is a fine lawn. As for the smocking itself – it may well outlive the gown, for small boys do enjoy a rough and tumble."

"Mrs Long, I really do not know what you are saying," said Mrs Bennet. "But we must, alas, continue with our preparations for the journey to Derbyshire. Kitty comes from Lyme tomorrow and we shall have all the business of readying her for the trip."

Mr Collins said that Kitty would find a young man at Pemberley and that there was bound to be a ball, for Lady Catherine, Mr Darcy's aunt, had written to him very recently saying she hoped the tradition of the New Year's Ball would be continued and the fact of a Mrs Darcy at Pemberley would not prevent it.

"Why should my Lizzy stop a ball?" cried Mrs Bennet. "But what are we to wear? And who is this young man, Mr Collins, I would like to know?"

Mr Collins was glad to impart the information that the young man was a Master Roper. He was a cousin of Lady Catherine and therefore of Mr Darcy and she intended to apply to Mr Darcy for an invitation to Master Roper, who would otherwise be alone at Christmas, for an invitation to Pemberley.

"Very thoughtful, I am sure," said Mary.

Mrs Bennet enquired into the prospects of Master Roper; and at the same time complained that Kitty would have nothing at all to wear for so grand an occasion as a ball at Pemberley.

"Master Roper, Mrs Bennet," said Mr Collins, "is Mr Darcy's heir."

"What can you mean by that?" cried Mrs Bennet, most disagreeably surprised by this information. "The son born to my own daughter Elizabeth will be Mr Darcy's heir."

"In the event of Mr Darcy's dying without a son and heir, Pemberley is in entail to Master Roper," Mr Collins explained. "Lady Catherine de Bourgh" – and here he bowed, as if that august personage had walked into the room – "Lady Catherine does not know why a family of the stature of the Darcys should go in for entail. It is not like Longbourn, you know."

"So we are thrown out of our home and to be doubly pitied," Mary said with some dryness. "We are not grand enough to do without an entail and that is somehow our fault for not being able to stay in the house we grew up in!"

"Rosings is not in entail," said Mr Collins, who had no desire to reply to Mary's charge. "Lady Catherine can rest assured that Miss de Bourgh will inherit Rosings."

After reiterating that from all he heard Master Roper was a personable young man, Mr Collins took his leave; and Mrs Long, when she had delivered instructions on the future preservation of the smock, did likewise.

# Ten

It happened every year at Pemberley in the week leading up to Christmas that Mr Darcy and a group of his friends travelled to his estates in Yorkshire where a hunting lodge was made ready for their occupation. Pheasants, blackcock, partridge and other game were the quarry; and in years past the party had been exclusively male, the wives of the huntsmen being expected to greet their spouses on their return with a range fired for boiling and stewing, and a hot spit for roasting in the rare event of a deer.

This year, however – and it pleased Elizabeth that it had been her doing – the wives were invited. Mr Bingley was one of the group; Jane, for all her energy and good nature, considered herself too far gone in her pregnancy to walk up the birds, as the other women eagerly looked forward to doing; and Georgiana Darcy came in her stead. Mr Bingley's sister Mrs Hurst and her husband were also guests; and the party was rounded by Elizabeth's uncle and aunt Gardiner. Of the latter two it could honestly be said that Mr Darcy had come to love them – indeed, as he often reminded them, laughing, if they had not brought their niece, the lovely Eliza, to Derbyshire on a visit, he might never have married at all! For all the sardonic wit of Miss Bingley and Mrs Hurst – who, as Elizabeth well knew, had done all they could to prevent her marriage to Mr Darcy – the friendship that had grown up between Mr Darcy and her aunt and uncle was real and strong. Miss Bingley might have jested that Elizabeth's relations would look ridiculous indeed in the long gallery, next to Mr Darcy's, and that he must make sure to have them painted and placed there; but Mr Darcy had responded to the challenge with the utmost gravity and had sworn he would commission an artist to come to Pemberley and execute a portrait of Elizabeth alone; and one, too, of Elizabeth with her aunt and uncle. This last when completed would hang near Mr Darcy's great-uncle the High Court Judge; a fact which Mr Darcy frequently announced; and, if Elizabeth had a dread of Miss Bingley's comments at the time of her Christmas visit, she also knew she could count on Darcy's contempt for the arrogance and condescension of Mr Bingley's sisters. She could only reflect with some gratification, as they came near to the lodge, that she had softened Darcy in this way as in so many others. He had taken pains to lose his fiery insolence. He followed his heart in his friendships these days, as he had in his choice of a wife.

The lodge was set in a rugged landscape, and Mr Gardiner, who was in the carriage with Elizabeth and Mrs Gardiner, took great interest in the rushing water they crossed, by means of a rustic bridge, in order to reach their destination. "There will be salmon there, I've no doubt," pronounced Mr Gardiner. "It has taken me close on a year, I confess, to learn to trust Mr Darcy; for there are many who hand out an invitation to an angler to fish their waters and then profess themselves astonished when he turns up. But your Darcy, my dear" – and he smiled at Elizabeth – "gave me permission to fish the streams at Pemberley the very first time we met; and he has not once reneged on his promise."

"I should hope not!" cried Mrs Gardiner. "Lizzy's cook has a fine way with trout and you have supplied the breakfast table at Pemberley more than once, sir!"

Whilst Elizabeth smiled at her aunt and uncle's pleasantries, she could not but admit to herself her extreme gratitude to the kindly pair for deciding to rent a house at Rowsley for the duration of the Christmas season. There were so many good reasons why Mr Wickham should not come to Pemberley as the guest of Mr Darcy and herself. It was Mr Wickham who had been, as Elizabeth recalled with agitation each time, the cause of her most glaring prejudices, for she had believed his account of cruel and unjust treatment at the

40

hands of Mr Darcy, when in fact Mr Darcy's generosity to Mr Wickham had been outstanding. Wickham was the son of the old Mr Darcy's estate manager; and had been promised a living, when the time came; but his debts and evil ways (all helped with kindness and patience by young Darcy after his father's death) had made it impossible for this living to be granted. Only after Elizabeth's wounding words to Mr Darcy on the occasion of his first – and unwelcome – proposal of marriage had drawn the truth, in a letter from the misjudged suitor, had she understood fully how nefarious the young protégé had been. Wickham had received from Darcy three thousand pounds! And this he had squandered, too. The fact of Elizabeth's having been partial to the young man at the time was also of considerable embarrassment to her.

Georgiana Darcy stepped from the door of the lodge to welcome the Gardiners and Elizabeth; and as she did so Elizabeth could not help but reflect on another good reason for her pleasure in Wickham's being at five miles' distance at the time of their festive celebrations. Wickham – as Darcy had told Elizabeth in the greatest confidence – had lured Georgiana to Ramsgate when she was a mere fifteen years old. With the connivance of her chaperone, he had taken the innocent girl, who quickly thought herself in love with him, with the intention of forcing an elopement, to a seaside hotel from which she had only escaped by appealing to Darcy for a seal of approval which he absolutely refused to give. Her fortune was thirty thousand pounds; and it was for this that Wickham hunted her. But Elizabeth was concerned, for Georgiana, that there had been no suitor since and that the young woman might still entertain bitter regrets over the whole affair. It would have been intolerable indeed, if this were the case, to entertain Lydia, Elizabeth's own sister, as a rival to her new sister, Georgiana.

As they alighted from the carriage, Elizabeth found the first opportunity to thank her aunt Gardiner for the tact demonstrated in renting rather than permitting Lydia and Mr Wickham to come to Pemberley.

"There was no stopping her coming north," said Mrs

Gardiner in her usual pleasant tone. "She says, to be reunited with her Mama, but I think to enjoy the New Year's Ball at Pemberley!"

Elizabeth had here to bite her lip and keep silent. She did not wish to admit that the first she had heard of the New Year's Ball had been from her sister Jane, only a few days before; and that her enquiries of Mr Darcy had resulted only in a yawn and a cocked eyebrow and the assertion that it was a boring custom previously run by his aunt Catherine and he was surprised Mrs Reynolds had not been rattling on about it to poor Eliza for weeks now.

"The ball is for Miss Georgiana Darcy," said Elizabeth – for so she had concluded: that if the occasion were already fixed, then she would make the best of it in hoping a young man might come forward for Georgiana. "It is not for Lydia's pleasure solely, I am sure!"

They were by this time approaching the door of the lodge. Mr Darcy stepped forward to greet his wife and her aunt and uncle; and Mr Gardiner was able to pursue his interest in the salmon lurking in the waters that flowed all round the lodge, making an island that was picturesque in the extreme.

"I shall not be deflected," said Mr Darcy as they went through into the hall and divested themselves of their wraps. "You may fish whenever you please, uncle Gardiner; but there is a greater challenge to be met on the moor tomorrow." And he proceeded, in the most civil of terms, to expound on the variety of game to be met on the Darcy Yorkshire estates.

# Eleven

The following day Elizabeth spent walking the moors; and as she went she reflected that the contrast with Pemberley, the range of mountains and the silence broken only by the becks that wound between hills almost devoid of trees, could give her a new perspective on her life and her position as the wife of Mr Darcy. Pemberley, with its fine arrangements of land and views from each window as well deliberated as a theatrical set, demanded of her in turn a part to play – here, she could, for the first time since her marriage, feel herself.

For this reason, Elizabeth had chosen to walk with the beaters rather than with the shots: as she had surmised, the men and boys from the village dispersed rapidly into brushwood and covert and she was left alone; and this, too, recalled to her the solitary walks she had taken in the park at Rosings, when, as a guest of her friend Charlotte and Mr Collins at the Hunsford parsonage, she had found herself confronted by the figure of Mr Darcy at every turn.

She was happy to have this day to herself; there was no doubt in that; but Elizabeth knew also that a surfeit of hours away from Mr Darcy's company could make her yearn for him as if the separation had been in weeks or months – and that, just as she enjoyed the solitude and the feelings that arose in her on contemplation of the romantic scenery and expanse of sky, so too could she have greeted the sight of Mr Darcy coming over the moor towards her with extreme joy. If only they could be solitary together sometimes! How wonderful that would be! But the fact of Mr Darcy's duties to his estates and men, and the proximity of a season of entertaining at Pemberley, made the possibility even more remote than was usual. A wild hope, that a distant figure on the side of the hill, descending precipitately towards her, could be Darcy after all – for Elizabeth hoped always that he would cast off his reserve more often and run to her from the pure desire of her company, as she did for the want of his – was soon dispelled by the increasing visibility of the figure as it approached. Elizabeth did not yet know the names or faces of many of those who cared for the Yorkshire estates, but she recognised this man as a gamekeeper, to whom she had been introduced that morning by her husband; and whom she had greeted, as she so often felt, with too little formality. It was still difficult for the new mistress of Pemberley – and of this estate too, she must suppose – to accept the obeisances given by those who worked on the land; and she recalled in particular the stiffness of this man's bow in response to her words of welcome.

The news brought by the gamekeeper was alarming – but, as Elizabeth discovered a guilt in herself for feeling – at least it did not concern Mr Darcy. Mrs Hurst, on ascending a mountain too speedily, had fallen and sprained her ankle. A pony and cart had been sent for, from the lodge. Mrs Hurst was adamant that her husband should continue with his day's shooting, and Mr Darcy asked if his wife would be gracious enough to accompany Mrs Hurst to the lodge and attend her there. Mr Darcy had asked him, the gamekeeper said in a solemn tone that had Elizabeth look away to prevent her from laughing, to inform Mrs Darcy that Mrs Gardiner had been most insistent that it should be she who would accompany the invalid; but Mr Darcy knew that Mrs Darcy would prefer her aunt to remain on the moor and enjoy the spectacle of the shoot with Mr Gardiner. Elizabeth showed her gratitude at Darcy's delicacy in wishing to let her know of her aunt's scrupulous kindness on this occasion – as on so many others – by wringing the hand of the gamekeeper, which only served to confuse him further. As they set off down the track, the pony and cart, with Mrs Hurst aboard, could be seen coming up towards them; and after the keeper had assisted them and the groom had been instructed to go carefully over the stony stretch of the road as they approached the lodge, they set off without too much discomfort on the part of Elizabeth's new patient.

Mrs Hurst had nothing but pleasant airs and kind thanks for Elizabeth's solicitude; and if she was in pain she took care to conceal it. For all her compliments, however, Elizabeth knew the feelings of her charge, temporarily disabled though she might be, were in all probability more distressing than any amount of physical unease. It had first been seen at Netherfield, the house rented by Mr Bingley near Longbourn, this curious blend of patronage and arrogance towards the Bennet girls on the part of Mr Bingley's sisters, Caroline and Mrs Hurst; and the cruel witticisms at the expense of her mother and her sister Jane had not gone unnoticed by Elizabeth. Remarks about *her*, as she correctly surmised, were made direct to Mr Darcy, where they received either an icy rejoinder or none at all, as they deserved.

There was no reason to suppose that the marriage of Elizabeth and Darcy would have changed the opinions of Mr Bingley's sisters on Elizabeth – or, indeed, on her sister Jane. For had not Caroline Bingley, as the sister of Mr Darcy's best friend, considered herself the future bride of Mr Darcy and his ten thousand a year? And had not her sister Jane married their brother Mr Bingley, who had in all certainty been intended for Miss Darcy? Marriage between Georgiana and Charles Bingley would have brought Pemberley a good deal closer to his sisters, as Elizabeth was very well aware; and she resolved, as she conversed with Mrs Hurst on the way back to the lodge, to keep her composure even if provoked.

"I dare say your mother and sisters will be visiting for Christmas," said Mrs Hurst. "Have they been to Pemberley before, dearest Lizzy?"

Elizabeth replied that they had not. She did not add that she much disliked being addressed in such familiar terms by Mrs Hurst, though it was conceivable that the fact of Jane being married to Mrs Hurst's brother did indeed make them connected.

"Ah, well, they must be looking forward to it immensely!"

cried Mrs Hurst, as the pony cart jolted over a rough patch of road and a silence was ensured for a while at least while Elizabeth tended the swollen ankle and the patient assured her she suffered hardly at all.

"You must be wondering where you will put them," said Mrs Hurst when they were on smoother ground. "There are so many traditions attached to an old house like Pemberley, you know, and it is so easy to make mistakes – and, quite unwittingly, cause offence."

Elizabeth replied that she had thought of the placing of the guests and that she and Mrs Reynolds were well satisfied with the arrangements.

"Tell me," cried Mrs Hurst, "apart from your mother and your sisters, will you invite your aunts? I am told you have an aunt who lives in Cheapside." And here Mrs Hurst gave a hearty laugh. "It is quite a way from Cheapside to Pemberley, to be sure. But we should all be sorry to hear she had come such a distance only to find herself lodged at Rowsley with Mrs Gardiner, like your sister Mrs Wickham."

Elizabeth's cheeks flamed; but as the lodge was now in sight through the trees she determined to rise as little as possible to Mrs Hurst's bait. She said in a measured tone that her London aunt was not coming to Pemberley and had never considered doing so; that her aunt Gardiner was in the habit of taking lodgings at Rowsley in order better to tour the area; and that her younger sister Lydia would find the amenities of Lambton of great use to her numerous children.

"There are no soldiers billeted there," said Mrs Hurst with a note of triumph. "I fear your sister Kitty will be hard put to amuse herself when she visits Lydia in Rowsley."

These insinuations proving almost too much for her, Elizabeth ordered the pony cart to stop and she alighted in the driveway to the lodge, saying she would call the servants to assist Mrs Hurst dismount. When she had done this, she returned to the cart and took the invalid's hand with the most cheerful of smiles.

"Oh, my dear Eliza, you are too kind," said Mrs Hurst. "Come up with me to my bedchamber while we wait for a doctor, I do beg you. I am so fretful left on my own with no one to prattle to."

Unwillingly Elizabeth agreed, and they made their way at a necessarily slow pace up the stairs.

"Here we are!" said Mrs Hurst as she paused on the landing outside Mr Darcy's room. "Come in here with me, my dear."

Elizabeth said she could see no reason to enter her husband's room. She had the unpleasant sensation that Mrs Hurst was watching her closely as she spoke; as if, very nearly, Mrs Hurst considered Elizabeth had something to hide, and was afraid to show it. Yet this, as Elizabeth knew, was plain nonsense. Anyone who wished could enter her own or Mr Darcy's rooms and see the evidence of their devotion and faithful love for each other – for Elizabeth's room bore all the marks of his constant occupancy, and his room was as bare as a bedchamber allocated to a bachelor guest before his arrival to stay. Whether at Pemberley or in the lodge in Yorkshire, this was invariably the case; and Elizabeth knew Mr Darcy's manservant had at first been surprised to find his master so seldom in his own quarters. But the truth was there for all to see: Mr Darcy used his room as a dressing-room only, and there were few couples even in these enlightened times who could say as much for the harmony of their conjugal relations.

Elizabeth asked Mrs Hurst why she should wish to enter Mr Darcy's room, when he was out on the moors and could not possibly be expected to be there. "And if by some miracle he *were* there," said Elizabeth, "he would be changing from his shooting-clothes. He would hardly expect us to walk in there."

"Ah, it was when dear Darcy was changing this morning that I heard him exclaim with surprise," cried Mrs Hurst. "The door was open and I was walking past. When I asked him what was the matter, he replied that he had just received a letter from his aunt, Lady Catherine de Bourgh."

"And what of it?"

"He confided in me directly that Lady Catherine intends

to bring another guest to Pemberley for Christmas," said Mrs Hurst with an even greater note of triumph than before. "I would have thought he'd have told you of an addition to the party, my dear Eliza."

"I did not have a chance to speak with Darcy before we went out walking," said Elizabeth, who instantly regretted having spoken these words.

"There is no need to apologise, Elizabeth. Many wives know even less of their husband's movements or intentions. I can assure you, the degree of close confidentiality between myself and Mr Hurst is most extraordinary."

Elizabeth could scarcely refrain from smiling, as Mr Hurst slept so soundly after dinner, before being carried up to bed and sleeping until wakened by the need for breakfast, that the actuality of an exchange of words was commonly considered, at any hour of the day, to be highly improbable between the couple.

"I am sure I will be informed of Lady Catherine's bringing another guest," said Elizabeth with a gravity which masked her true feelings for Mr Bingley's sister. "And now, if I may, I will assist you to your room and retire to mine."

"Very well. But I am amazed, my dear Lizzy, that you take no interest in the imminent arrival at Pemberley of its heir."

"What are you saying? I do not understand."

"Lady Catherine befriends a distant cousin – of hers and of Mr Darcy's. He is Master Thomas Roper, and by entail he stands to inherit all the Darcy estates and wealth if Fitzwilliam Darcy should take leave of the world without male issue."

"I welcome any relative of my husband's," said Elizabeth. She did not know how she proceeded to assist Mrs Hurst to her room without misadventure – but this she achieved, glad to show presence of mind when it came to pulling up a sofa, and laying the invalid's foot most tenderly there.

# Twelve

The return of the shooting party having been delayed by a particularly fine display by Mr Gardiner – and, for all his modesty, the good man's cheeks glowed at the compliments on the number of birds he brought down – there was no time before dinner in which Elizabeth could summon Mr Darcy to her side and ask the meaning of Mrs Hurst's strange communication. He went to his room to change; and for the first time in their marriage Elizabeth hesitated by the door and then walked away rather than call for her husband to open and fly into his arms. The letter from Lady Catherine was now the denizen of Mr Darcy's room. Furthermore, the denizen was secret, for he had not divulged its existence to her. Elizabeth wondered how long the letter had been in her husband's possession, for, whatever Mrs Hurst might say, that it had arrived this morning, Elizabeth did not see by what means it could have come. No express passed the lodge, which was remote from the nearest road. No, Mr Darcy must have brought the letter with him from Pemberley. He had then elected to keep silent on the subject of the contents – to his wife at least – for, as Elizabeth thought with some bitterness, he had confided in Mrs Hurst at the most mild of promptings.

Mrs Hurst now called Elizabeth to her room; and, under the pretext of demonstrating the injury to her foot, looked closely at the new chatelaine of Pemberley. What she saw must have provided some satisfaction, for she laughed – before concealing her laughter under the pretence of pain.

"Is not the arch of my foot exceedingly high, cousin Elizabeth? They say a high arch is a sign of breeding. I have not been able to discern the height of *your* instep, hidden beneath your gown in such pretty slippers! You have seen enough of *my* lower extremities, dear Lizzy – now let me see yours."

"I have matters to attend to," said Elizabeth, who had no intention of displaying herself in this fashion to Mrs Hurst; and she made to leave the room once more.

"There have been exquisitely high arches in the Darcy family," Mrs Hurst called out; "and they come directly from Lady Anne Darcy, so I am told. I am sorry we are not permitted to see your feet, Elizabeth – for I can think of nothing more regrettable than a flat-footed heir to Pemberley!"

In her enjoyment of this latest sally, Mrs Hurst forgot herself enough to attempt to place a foot on the ground; and, as she did so, she cried out, lost her footing altogether and subsided on the floor beside the sofa. Her calls for aid went unheeded by Elizabeth, who took time, at least, to call back up the stairs to Mr Bingley's sister, in tones both consolatory and high-spirited.

"Lizzy! I am on the floor – am I to crawl up alone?" came the voice of Mrs Hurst as Elizabeth descended further.

"I fear so," the answer returned clearly. "For there is a saying, Mrs Hurst, that you would do well to recall as you try."

"And what can that be?"

"Why, 'Pride comes before a Fall'," said Elizabeth loud and clear, and fearing nothing from the glance of a maid who came out on the landing to see where the noise was from. Then, still holding the information the sister of her husband's dearest friend had just handed to her, of the unexpected addition to the Christmas party at Pemberley, she went to the sitting-room and tried to compose her thoughts.

Her mood was soon sombre.

The existence of an heir to Pemberley, unknown to Elizabeth, produced in her a contrariety of emotions. There was no reason – of course there was not – to keep from her the facts of an entail. Indeed, there was also no reason to bring

50

the matter to her attention, either. Any mention might have proved indelicate in the extreme. Yet Elizabeth felt that she was precarious now, for the first time since she had plighted her troth with Mr Darcy. Was he as content as he seemed, with the love he so frequently and ardently announced to her? Was being a wife enough, for him and for Pemberley? Was she not already a failed mother?

Elizabeth resolved to put these ideas at the back of her mind; and for the sake of her aunt and uncle Gardiner – the latter beaming throughout the meal at the sincere flattery paid him by Mr Hurst and Mr Darcy – she was at her most light-hearted and charming. Darcy, too, threw her such a succession of amorous looks, quickly stifled always for fear of interception but detectable by Elizabeth, that she soon wondered at her feelings earlier. There could be little doubt that the reason for Darcy's reticence on the subject of Master Roper was similar to her own some time before at Pemberley, when she had found herself asking for the favour of Mrs Bennet and her sisters' company at Christmas. Darcy might feel that a strange young man as a late addition to the party would cause a constraint for Elizabeth with her own family. And that Lady Catherine had demanded he be invited! Darcy would know Elizabeth had guessed at the animosity of his aunt towards her: from her meeting with Lady Catherine at Longbourn and the extreme insolence of the latter in asking direct questions as to her intentions regarding Mr Darcy as a possible husband, there could be little doubt about the extent of her disapproval of the new Mrs Darcy. And Darcy must know, though it had never been said between them, that Elizabeth had also guessed at the content of some of the previous letters from Lady Catherine to her nephew. That they were abusive of her to the utmost degree she doubted not at all. She loved Darcy for noting her sense of dread at Lady Catherine's impending arrival to stay at Pemberley for the first time since their marriage. He had clearly decided to save the information that his aunt had taken the liberty of inviting their young cousin, for their return to Pemberley from the lodge. It was a measure of his good will and happy humour that he had forgiven Lady Catherine – who had had to cease her abusiveness on the subject of Mrs Darcy in order to be allowed to Pemberley once more – and this same feeling of good will lay behind his decision to keep the news of Master Roper from Elizabeth.

Mrs Hurst and Mrs Gardiner were engaged in a discussion on the merits of some of the contemporary painters in England. "I cannot see why Mr Darcy delays in having your niece's portrait done! I can only wish Sir Joshua Reynolds were still alive and able to paint at Pemberley! What a fine picture he would have made of Lizzy!"

As Mrs Gardiner made no reply to this, Mrs Hurst continued: "I have heard the paints he used are most unreliable. Mrs Fisher tells me she has faded already!"

Again, Mrs Gardiner could think of no response to this. Both Elizabeth and Darcy had heard the exchange and they smiled at each other the length of the table. Elizabeth knew Darcy was keen for a portrait of her, but she had so far desisted, on grounds that she had better things to do than pose in order to gratify her own vanity.

"Dear Jane, as you may know, Mrs Gardiner, has agreed to a portrait. My brother Charles Bingley is quite delighted! Jane will wear a white dress with green ornaments, she tells me."

"I know green to be Jane's favourite colour," Mrs Gardiner responded with warmth.

"She will wait until after the birth of their second child," said Mrs Hurst. "She will be painted with the children, I have no doubt; and Mr Bingley too, if he wishes it."

"It will be a fine picture," said Mrs Gardiner.

"Oh yes," cried Mrs Hurst, for the table was quiet now, Mr Gardiner and Mr Hurst having exhausted the topic of the merits of blackcock versus tufted grouse. "It is always so much better for the lady of a house to pose with her children around her – and the house in the background, that cannot be bettered as a composition, for it says in so many words that the continuity of the line is assured and the estate will remain within the family!"

Mr Darcy rose at this, scowling dreadfully. Too late,

Elizabeth rose also, so the ladies could leave the dining-room to the gentlemen; and, as she rose, she felt the pitying eyes of Mrs Hurst on her. From a family such as the Bennets, where five daughters and Mrs Bennet had seldom, if ever, left the dining-room to Mr Bennet alone – for he preferred the library and would often go in there to escape the prattling of his younger daughters at table – it was particularly hard for Elizabeth to gauge the exact moment of needful departure for the ladies. Several times at Pemberley she had felt the eyes of Mr Darcy on her, and had wondered at the intensity of his scrutiny, only to realise with shame that the hour was late and there were wives and daughters still at table who should long ago have left the men to their port.

Once away from the dining-room, Elizabeth led her aunt and Mrs Hurst with as much composure as she could muster to her boudoir. Tea was brought in; and Mrs Hurst declared herself very well satisfied with her visit to Mr Darcy's Yorkshire estates.

"He was here as a young boy a good deal," said Mrs Hurst, "so my brother tells me. It may explain the love he has for the *picturesque*" – and here she darted another glance at Elizabeth. "A perfect place for a child, do not you agree, Mrs Gardiner, and such a pity the place is so little used!"

The hour wound on, but tonight the gentlemen did not come away from their port, and Mrs Gardiner, declaring herself fatigued by the fresh air of the moors, said she was going up to bed. Mrs Hurst wished to do likewise; and aunt and niece assisted her up the stairs. Announcing that she would see the doctor tomorrow when he came, but there had really been no need to send for him, for she was famous for mending, even on the hunting field, so very much faster after a fall than anyone else, Mrs Hurst went into her room and closed the door.

Mrs Gardiner, with the warmest expressions of love and gratitude for the delightful visit that she and uncle Gardiner were enjoying, kissed Elizabeth and went to her room.

Elizabeth lay a long time awake in bed, before her eyes closed and she entered a fitful sleep. Several times she awoke – but Mr Darcy did not come.

PART TWO

# Part Two

# Thirteen

Mrs Bennet's concerns, on the last day of preparation before going north to Derbyshire, were with the contents of a letter she had received from a distant cousin on her father's side, Colonel Kitchiner. As neither Kitty, who was much taken up with the future possibility of there being a regiment stationed at Rowsley or thereabouts, nor Mary, who complained already that she would not be able to find her way round the library at Pemberley, was in a fit state to hear Mrs Bennet's confidences on the matter, Mrs Long was summoned for the last time to Meryton Lodge and offered tea.

"My dear Mrs Bennet," said Mrs Long, "how can you find time to entertain visitors when all your thoughts must be with your daughter, and her condition? With Jane, I mean" – for Mrs Bennet shifted in her chair and made to tuck away a letter at this. "There must be news of a very significant nature," Mrs Long permitted herself, "and I can only hope that your journey north will not be adversely affected."

"Not at all!" cried Mrs Bennet, opening out the letter and folding it again. "Unexpected certainly – but, I have to say, not entirely untimely. It is from my cousin, Colonel Kitchiner."

Mrs Long allowed that she had never heard tell of Colonel Kitchiner.

"That is very probable. He has been away at war and is now retired at Uplyme. A most entrancing spot, as I know well. For I went there – with poor Mr Bennet – on the occasion of Lydia's going to Weymouth, if you remember."

"A most unfortunate occasion," said Mrs Long. "It is to be hoped there are no soldiers to be found in Derbyshire –

for Kitty has every appearance of going the same way as her sister."

"Lydia is married," said Mrs Bennet simply, but not without reflecting that her friend's candour had greatly increased since the death of Mr Bennet. "And I may say that I have intentions of a similar nature. Can there be anything ill-considered in marrying a soldier?"

Mrs Long was as startled as her friend had intended her to be. "Mrs Bennet, do you mean this? I pray you, recollect yourself."

At this moment the maid came in and the tea was removed. Mrs Bennet offered a cordial, which was accepted, and the maid withdrew.

"Colonel Kitchiner writes that he hopes to renew my acquaintance when he visits his sister — a cousin of mine as she must be — who lives in Manchester. He goes north in a few days' time and spends Christmas with her there."

"Indeed," cried Mrs Long, "but I fail to see that you must feel yourself obliged to enter the matrimonial state because of this. Mr Bennet has been dead no more than nine months."

"Mr Bennet would approve greatly," Mrs Bennet replied with a stiffness of manner which was not conducive to Mrs Long's continuing this train of thought. "You will recall that Longbourn was entailed into the male line."

"Certainly," said Mrs Long, "it would be unusual in the extreme were anyone in the neighbourhood to fail to recall this. But your son-in-law, Mr Fitzwilliam Darcy, has settled you here most comfortably at Meryton Lodge."

"For my lifetime only," said Mrs Bennet, this time in a low tone.

"But for how much longer after that would you require it?" cried Mrs Long, who went on to profess herself baffled by Mrs Bennet today.

"My father, who was an attorney in Meryton, as you well know, my dear Mrs Long, was unable to leave me more than four thousand pounds. His partner, the father of Colonel Kitchiner, was enabled to do likewise for his son. Colonel Kitchiner's idea — and I may say it is not entirely unappealing

– is for a joining of these fortunes; and he has even had the foresight to suggest that my unmarried daughters, his 'young cousins', as he delightfully terms it, should come into the sum of eight thousand pounds at his demise – as well as his house in Uplyme. For" – and here Mrs Bennet wiped a tear from her eye – "for at my death they will scarcely be able to count on Meryton Lodge."

"It is certainly generous of Colonel Kitchiner," said Mrs Long after a pause for reflection in which she wished the ailing and selfish Mr Long dead and buried and herself taking the air at Uplyme. "So you have accepted – or, my dear Mrs Bennet, will you do so soon?"

"On no account will I accept," said Mrs Bennet, to the further surprise of Mrs Long.

"But Mrs Bennet, why not? You will earn the everlasting gratitude of your daughters – for I accede that it may well be almost impossible for them to find husbands. With so small a fortune to look forward to," Mrs Long added, just in time to escape the eye of Mrs Bennet. "What can possibly hold you back from this agreeable and sensible proposition?"

"Perhaps," said Mrs Bennet, "there is a reason, Mrs Long, why I draw back from the suggestion."

Mrs Long looked at her friend with incredulous solicitude, but said nothing.

"I am the mother of Mrs Darcy, of Pemberley," said Mrs Bennet, colouring.

"You are," said Mrs Long, "and of Jane Bingley and three other girls, as we know."

"I cannot commit myself to a marriage without the appro-bation of my daughter and son-in-law. It would be most awk-ward. I am astonished that you do not see this, Mrs Long."

"But – it was you, Mrs Bennet, who announced that your mind was made up."

"Not at all. I asked whether you thought it ill considered to marry a soldier."

"But this is a colonel!" cried Mrs Long. "And the war is over, Mrs Bennet. I believe you must be most fatigued, in your preparations for your journey to Pemberley."

"Ah, my nerves, Mrs Long, have been so terribly affected since the death of Mr Bennet! And I cannot know how my Lizzy, who was quite her father's favourite, as you may recall, would ever take to my remarrying."

"Elizabeth would wish you well, I am sure. And she will be aware that her younger sisters will be well cared for. You worry too much, Mrs Bennet – and Elizabeth has other matters on her mind, I have no doubt, besides your matrimonial affairs."

"And what might they be?" enquired Mrs Bennet.

"She is in a different time of life to yours," was all Mrs Long would give in reply.

Mrs Bennet proceeded to complain of Mrs Long's heartlessness at approving a marriage when thirty years had passed since she had set eyes on the groom. She repeated several times that she must wait for the approval of her daughter Lizzy before committing herself to the match, when the door opened and Mr Collins was shown in.

"Mr Collins!" said Mrs Bennet, with as much composure as she could muster.

Mr Collins bowed and presented his apologies for calling on the eve of the departure of Mrs Bennet and her daughters for Pemberley. It was seen by Mrs Long and Mrs Bennet that he clasped a small box, made of inlaid wood, in his hand.

"It is merely a token, a Christmas wish," said Mr Collins, bowing again and holding out the box. "It will not impress by its presumption, but may bring a happy memory of summer days."

Mrs Bennet took the box and opened it. A collection of dusty rose petals and the remains of other flowers gave off a faint haze.

"I have a cold in the nose, or I am sure I could detect the fragrance," cried Mrs Long.

"From the garden at Longbourn," said Mr Collins with evident pride. "My dear Charlotte and I gathered them when the sun was high, on St John's Eve. Indeed, it is said of young women on midsummer eve that they have only to look in the mirror and they will see the face of their future husband. Charlotte of course had already done me the honour of becoming my wife –"

Here Kitty came in, the maid and Mary just behind her. "Mama, you must tell Mary there is no room in the coach for such a quantity of books. How can I put in the ball dresses I must take in the event of a ball? Where shall we sit, if the dresses are not to be crushed?"

"A ball at Pemberley?" cried Mr Collins. "Indeed, there will be a ball at Pemberley. Every year on New Year's Eve. I cannot give my word, my dear Kitty, that you will find a husband as maids are wont to do at midsummer" – and here Mr Collins attempted a twinkle in the eye that sent Mary bolting from the room – "but I can assure you that all the young men of family in the district will be invited. Lady Catherine de Bourgh will see to that!"

"My daughter Mrs Darcy will arrange the ball this year," said Mrs Bennet. "And now – as we have so short a time until we leave . . ."

Mr Collins took the box from Mrs Bennet's hand and made as if to pronounce a sacrament over it. "You will be kind enough to give this to Mrs Darcy, with my kindest regards," said Mr Collins.

"The box is for Lizzy?" said Mrs Long.

Mr Collins bowed once more. "My dear cousin Elizabeth will find tender memories of childhood return to her. To think" – Mr Collins turned to embrace Mrs Bennet, Mrs Long and Kitty by opening his arms wide – "to think how mistaken my dear Charlotte and I proved to be, when Elizabeth came as our guest to Hunsford parsonage."

"Mistaken?" said Mrs Bennet, drawing herself up. "How so?"

"We were certain that Colonel Fitzwilliam, Lady Catherine's cousin, then a guest at Rosings, would propose marriage to Elizabeth. We found Colonel Fitzwilliam the pleasantest man."

The maid came in and said the coach was at the door.

"Heavens!" cried Mrs Bennet. "I am hardly ready at all!"

"Mr Darcy has considerable patronage in the church,"

said Mrs Long. "You must be glad the colonel came to nothing."

Mrs Bennet, who showed her guests the door, kept them in the hall long enough to make strong objection to Mrs Long's remark. "And what is wrong with a colonel, I would like to know? There is a colonel in my own family and I hope he is good enough for my daughter Mrs Darcy."

"And how should that arise?" said Mrs Long as Mr Collins stood still without opening his lips.

"Colonel Kitchiner will call on us at Pemberley, when he leaves Manchester after visiting his sister," said Mrs Bennet on a note of triumph, for she could no longer conceal her excitement from anyone. "And I expect Mr and Mrs Darcy to receive him most genially."

"Colonel Kitchiner?" said Mr Collins, who now wore a frown across his forehead. "I think I have heard the name before."

"Very likely," said Mrs Bennet. "He is received everywhere."

Mr Collins continued to frown; and to say several times that he had heard the name before, and he thought Colonel Kitchiner had been to Rosings.

"There you are!" said Mrs Bennet. "Lady Catherine, who will naturally recognise the colonel when he comes to Pemberley, will have many topics to discuss with him."

But Mr Collins continued to frown, and to mutter; and only the imminent departure of the Bennet family, and his own necessity of pointing out that the little inlaid box must perforce contain so many fewer blooms than would have been gathered in the garden at Rosings, led to the dispersal of the company.

"Lady Catherine will understand there is not the space for a wide variety of roses at Longbourn" were the last words of Mr Collins.

# Fourteen

Elizabeth's spirits were much restored on her return to Pemberley from Yorkshire by Mr Darcy's admission that his ill humour at the lodge could be ascribed to the manners of Mrs Hurst, and to a burning desire to be alone with his wife, uninterrupted by the presence of others, however pleasant aunt and uncle Gardiner might be.

She had cause to remember, too, her first impressions of the man she had married; that he had a very satirical eye, and if she did not begin by being impertinent herself she should soon grow afraid of him; and she had to confess to herself that the importance and duties attached to Mr Darcy, combined with what he termed his "resentfulness" – that he would not change his opinion once he had taken a decision to censure someone – had quenched her own natural impertinence a good deal. Was she not her father's daughter, the daughter of Mr Bennet, whose vision of the world was that neighbours were there to be made sport of; and what was oneself other than an object of their sport? Elizabeth feared she had been too much in thrall to her husband since their marriage – and, whilst she had no desire to mock the master of Pemberley, a man she loved distractedly, she considered it now timely to give vent to her feelings on the subject of Mrs Hurst. This was made all the easier by Mr Darcy's opening up after dinner, as Georgiana sketched by the fire and Elizabeth sat at her embroidery.

"I cannot imagine how Mrs Hurst can entertain herself so well, with so little in her head," said Darcy – and Elizabeth could feel that he smiled at her as he spoke and that he wished to please her – for Darcy was not known to discuss the character, foibles or otherwise, of anyone connected with so dear a friend as Charles Bingley.

"She has Mr Hurst's snores to contend with," said Elizabeth lightly, "which must be like living in a perpetual thunderstorm. No wonder she mistakes spite for wit – both come at the speed of lightning and the rumbling in the background confuses her."

"She will not be here for our Christmas party at least," said Darcy.

"Then you shall not find yourself resentful throughout the festivities," said Elizabeth in the same light tone. "You will be as happy to see Charles Bingley as I shall be happy to be with Jane; and that will make up the entire party from Barlow."

Georgiana, on hearing this, laid down her sketch-pad and came over to the sofa where Elizabeth plied her needle, and put her arms around her neck.

"Oh, Lizzy, can you forgive me?" And, rising, she ran over to Darcy's high-backed chair and perched on a stool at his feet. "As I walked along the road to the village today – "

"Yes, Georgiana," said Darcy, whose difference of more than ten years in age seemed all the more pronounced for Georgiana's sudden affectation of childishness. "What have you done now? You have brought a new little kitten into the house and daren't tell Eliza of it, is that it?"

"Oh no, Darcy. I saw Miss Bingley walking down the road."

"Miss Bingley?" It was Elizabeth's turn to make the interrogation.

"Her phaeton had a wheel loose and was at the blacksmith's."

"But what is Miss Bingley doing here at all?" Elizabeth said; and then saw Darcy's brow darken, for she had not spoken kindly.

"Why, she stays with Charles and Jane," cried Georgiana. "She came to Pemberley to revisit the scene of her happiest days – so she informed me. You said, Elizabeth, that she was likely to come north for the season."

"It was mentioned, yes," Elizabeth allowed.

"So what harm is there in all this?" asked Darcy; and he gently indicated to his sister that she return to her seat by the fire. "Are we all to tremble because Caroline Bingley visits her brother and takes a ride in the phaeton in the direction of Pemberley?"

"No, Darcy – I knew you would think nothing of it. I invited Miss Bingley – dear Caroline – to stay over Christmas. That is all I have to tell you, and" – this said defiantly in the silence which ensued – "at least Miss Bingley is not like her sister, Mrs Hurst."

"No, much worse," said Elizabeth; "and I do think, Georgiana, that you could apply to me before you issue invitations for Christmas." She rose, cheeks burning, and said something to the effect that it was time to go to bed.

"No, no, my sweet Eliza!" cried Darcy, who appeared determined to recapture the good humour of the earlier part of the evening. "We shall certainly not end on this note!" And he rose also, to clasp Elizabeth by the hand and draw her to his side. "We shall play a new game to tide us over the coming season," said he. "Georgiana, do you have your card and colours?"

"What am I to do with them?" demanded his sister, still refusing to look at Elizabeth.

"We'll have a game of Pemberley," said Elizabeth laughing, for she had divined Mr Darcy's intentions. "You may start with a fine card of my mother, Mrs Bennet."

"And do not neglect an excellent likeness of my aunt, Lady Catherine," put in Mr Darcy.

"And Miss de Bourgh and Miss Kitty Bennet together . . ."

But, as Darcy and Elizabeth laughed and stood close in the long gallery, they found themselves, when next they turned towards the fire, alone together. Georgiana, scattering her pad and colours, had fled to her room.

"She was not invited, even, to make a likeness of Wickham," said Darcy gravely – and, for all the touch of cruelty that might be found in the remark, Elizabeth could not keep herself from showing her appreciation of it with a smile and an embrace. For was not Wickham – banished from

Pemberley and from the patronage of Mr Darcy so many years ago, only to attempt to seduce Miss Georgiana Darcy for her thirty thousand pounds – was not Wickham, who continued his scandalous career by eloping with Elizabeth's own sister Lydia, one of the chief components of Elizabeth's dread of the coming Christmas party? He would be at Rowsley, after all, with his wife and family – and many a night had Elizabeth lain awake and thought of the unpleasantness for poor Georgiana in all this.

"And now we will need a playing card of Miss Bingley too," said Elizabeth softly, as they mounted the stairs and a footman came after them to extinguish the lights.

But Mr Darcy said there was no need to design a card of Miss Bingley, for he had no desire to play with her at all.

# Fifteen

The next day was the last before the arrival of the guests at Pemberley. Elizabeth found herself increasingly grateful for the spirit of love and complicity that reigned between herself and Darcy; indeed, she owned that she had feared she would not be able to manage the occasion without the support and understanding given so freely by him, and that Christmas had seemed to her, in Yorkshire, too great a mountain to scale. Because she was accustomed to the company of Georgiana, Elizabeth confided her thoughts to her, as they walked through the park; and perhaps, distracted as she was, it took longer than it would naturally have done for her to note the silence of Miss Darcy on this and all other subjects. They stopped by a bower built by a stream, and sat down to rest, and still Elizabeth voiced her preoccupations concerning the coming season.

"You have had the benefit of the practical knowledge and skills of Mrs Reynolds since you were a child, my dear Georgiana. She is the most charming of women; the most effective of housekeepers. Yet I own I feel sometimes a total ignoramus compared to her. Where are people to sleep, when they come? Which bedroom is suitable for my mother and which for the young bachelor Lady Catherine brings with her? What shall we eat, three times a day? Should orders be given to kill the goose? Or do we wait until the New Year? And the ball! Shall we have sherbet and wine, and how will the lemonade be procured? Will the musicians arrive on time, in case of snowfall or stormy weather? You see how my poor mind is taken up, my dear sister."

Miss Darcy did not reply, and Elizabeth ran on: "I feel for

my mother now that I am in charge of an establishment. I own I used to mock her – indeed we all did – for making such a to-do over the dishes and the entertainment we offered to neighbours – and I have to say my father had a wicked tongue when it came to my mother's arrangements and the like. He would tell her to serve nothing at all to certain of the visitors, and Jane and I would laugh! But now I see that to be responsible for a house takes away a great amount of the enjoyment of life." And here Elizabeth drew herself up and laughed. "How I run on! I am like Mrs Bennet in this respect too! But I know you understand – and my happiness at the understanding of your dear brother is all I could ever have hoped for. Pemberley is on so much greater a scale than Longbourn, and there is so much to learn!"

Georgiana said she was sure the staff at Pemberley would give all assistance to Elizabeth when it was needed; and she suggested further that they walk up through the wood to the tower. "I have not heard that you have had time to visit the tower since you came to Pemberley. We played there as children. It is a magical place for children." Here Georgiana stopped and coloured.

"My dear Georgiana," said Elizabeth, for she saw that some influence had been at play on the girl, but she could not see whose, "I beg you not to suffer embarrassment when you talk of children in my presence. No one loves children more than I, and Nature will provide for us. I feel" – and here Elizabeth faltered, for she was unsure of Georgiana's response to a subject necessarily so intimate, but also, alas, so important to the family – "nay, I know, that the greater anxiety becomes in a woman when she contemplates the bearing of children, the less likely it will be that she will present her husband with a child. My sister Jane has told me this many times."

But – "I had no intention of prying," Georgiana said crossly; and now Elizabeth knew her to be in an ill humour; and ashamed, too, very probably, at her own actions of the previous day, for she had been wrong to invite Miss Bingley without the agreement of the mistress of Pemberley, and surely she knew it.

They walked up a wooded hill and soon found themselves on an eminence where a tower, designed in the days of Queen Bess and the other great Bess, of Hardwick, commanded a wide view of the landscape. Elizabeth exclaimed at the sight of Pemberley, quite small in the park from this height, and remarked that they had climbed higher than she thought. "Now I see the village in its entirety for the first time," she said. "How well laid out it is! Your father, the late Mr Darcy, had the welfare of his workers much at heart – this much I have heard from everyone on the estate."

"He cared for everyone equally," said Georgiana, who now showed some animation in her voice. "It was the kindness of his nature which deceived him when it came to the son of his bailiff, Mr Wickham. He gave no credence to the proposition that some are born evil and some good. He believed all could be ascribed to the nurturing of the soul, the rearing of the child. There was none like him in the country, so I have been told, and he is much mourned here."

"Yes, but your brother Mr Darcy is revered for his enlightened spirit also," said Elizabeth quickly. "Why, I recall my first visit to Pemberley – with my aunt and uncle Gardiner, we came as tourists simply – and Mrs Reynolds, who conducted us through the house, spoke of your brother in the same vein."

"My brother has sins to atone for," was all Miss Darcy would give in reply to Elizabeth's encomium. "Now please permit me to show you the tower. The design, as you may see, is of a four-leafed clover. If you walk round it entirely, it will become clear to you. Here it was that the imprisoned Queen of Scotland was taken, to watch the hunt as it went over that hill and down the dale."

Elizabeth professed her interest and astonishment at the historical site and romantic associations depicted by Miss Darcy – but her mind raced and she felt her heart pound at her own insensitivity. "I have taken into no account that my fears for the season at Pemberley are as nothing in comparison with poor Georgiana's; I have fretted over the coming presence of Mr Wickham, certainly, but I have not refused him entry to Pemberley, and that I should most definitely have done. The poor child! It was never said by Darcy quite how far Wickham's seduction had gone, by the time Darcy came to rescue his sister from Mrs Younge's establishment at Ramsgate – yet how she must fear and detest the vile Wickham, and how much of her affection and confidence I must myself have lost!"

Thus ran Elizabeth's thoughts, which caused her to blush dreadfully and to wish herself a thousand miles from the Scottish Queen's tower and the presence of Georgiana Darcy. As she stood, in apparent contemplation of Pemberley and its environs – her own home now, a place which she had hoped to make the home of her new sister also, and how she had betrayed that trust! – a group of children led by a young man of twenty-two or thereabouts became visible in a clearing in the wood beneath them.

"Ah, there is Mr Gresham," said Georgiana, who smiled and waved and received a greeting in return. The children halted and stared up at Mrs Darcy and Miss Darcy on the eminence above them.

"The children of the men who work here," said Elizabeth, for she felt satisfaction at recognising some of those who received her gifts in the village. "And who is Mr Gresham?"

"Oh, Lizzy," cried Georgiana, who seemed quite to have recovered her spirits, "I have spoiled my brother's secret! I shall tell you no more!"

"How can Mr Gresham be Darcy's secret?" exclaimed Elizabeth, relieved in the extreme that the expected presence of her poor sister Lydia's husband Mr Wickham had not upset the girl too much. "I do not recall any talk of a Mr Gresham!"

"Now you leave me no choice but to explain to you," said Georgiana, for the young man detached himself from the group and came up through the trees nimbly, eschewing the path. "He will wonder that you do not already know the position he will fill at Pemberley."

Before Georgiana had time to expound on this, Mr Gresham was standing beside them and bowing shyly to Mrs Darcy.

He was come to catalogue the famous library at Pemberley, at the request of Mr Fitzwilliam Darcy. As his origins were from hereabouts – he was the son of the present bailiff at Pemberley and had been raised on the estate, receiving an education which enabled him to continue his studies at the University of Oxford – Mr Darcy had done him the considerable honour of choosing him, rather than another more experienced librarian, for the task.

"Mr Darcy informed me, Madam, that it was your father, Mr Bennet, who had drawn his attention to the chaotic state of the library at Pemberley. It is in his memory, Mr Darcy instructs me, that he wishes a new annexe to be built, and craftsmen are even now engaged in engraving Mr Bennet's name and favourite saying – I believe it is from Ovid – in gold on the portal above the entrance to this new section of the library. Have I spoken wrongly?" Mr Gresham added in confusion, as Elizabeth turned away and wiped a tear from her eye. "I hope and trust, Mrs Darcy, that I have not offended in any way."

"Not at all," said Elizabeth, turning and smiling at the young librarian. "You have inadvertently given away the secret of Mr Darcy's gift to me."

"But surely, Lizzy, you heard the carpenters at work all this week," said Georgiana, laughing and taking Elizabeth's arm as they walked down the path together, Mr Gresham leaping down to rejoin the children. "Is it really such a surprise to you?"

Elizabeth owned that it was. "There is always something going on at Pemberley."

# Sixteen

Elizabeth's first wish, since hearing from Georgiana of the kindness and generosity of Darcy's gift to her, was to find him and thank him. How thoughtful of her feelings, how cognisant of the sense of loss of her father, whom she mourned so intensely and discreetly, a grief seen by Darcy but, from delicacy, never commented on, as she now knew – how tender in the concept of immortality bestowed on Mr Bennet by his name and most favoured sayings inscribed at Pemberley!

Elizabeth was hard pressed to recall when she had been so much moved by a gesture, from him. She resolved to lose the prejudice she felt – almost insurmountably at times – against his family, and those friends, the sisters of Charles Bingley, whom he had known before meeting her. She would forget the comment, made on more than one occasion by Miss Bingley, that a portrait of Mrs Bennet and her antecedents would prove a fine addition to the portrait gallery at Pemberley; and she would forget the tone in which this arch suggestion was made.

Darcy had designed the construction of the new wing to the library, it was now evident, to meet the time of the arrival of both their families and friends. Mrs Bennet – though Elizabeth drew back from imagining fully the effect of this tribute on her mother and the extent of her gratitude – would feel herself welcomed here, her husband's memory enshrined in the very part of the house which, at Longbourn, had caused her the greatest annoyance; and Elizabeth's eyes filled with tears of undimmed memory at the picture of her father, exasperated by his wife and younger daughters, taking refuge so constantly among his books. The marked reference to Mr Bennet's learning might keep Lady Catherine de Bourgh from the worst excesses of superiority – so Elizabeth dreamed and hoped, at least, as she sought Darcy up and down the expanses of Pemberley – and it seemed clearer to her as she went that this might be a strong reason for the haste in preparing a new catalogue for the library, all done "at the request of Mr Bennet". Her dear husband showed in this way that he would brook no continuation of the insolence and hauteur from his aunt, demonstrated both to Elizabeth and her mother on the famous occasion of her visit to Longbourn to discover Elizabeth's intentions in marrying Darcy; and to inform her that Miss de Bourgh had long been the intended bride of her cousin Fitzwilliam, a betrothal agreed with Lady Anne Darcy at the birth of Lady Catherine's daughter.

No, this must be the reason – and Elizabeth's heart gave a burst of joy – so much so, that on glimpsing Mrs Reynolds, who had some question of her preferences for the dinner on the following day, when all the party would be assembled, she took refuge in a small ante-room, seldom used, which lay between the long gallery and the library – whence her eager steps were bent – and concealed herself behind the door. There would be time enough for talk of hare soup and pheasant. Now, more than ever in all her year of marriage with Darcy, was the moment to find him and say she knew the secret of the library; that she had been blind not to have seen the work carried on there already, but had thought it simple repairs; that she had met Mr Gresham and understood that the late Mr Darcy's spirit of benevolent enlightenment, which had obtained for the odious Mr Wickham all the education and patronage he could desire, lived still in his son, this time to be rewarded by the evident honesty and sincerity of Mr Gresham. All this Elizabeth knew she must say; and, having searched everywhere for Darcy, knew also that he must be in the very sanctum designed around her father: there, fittingly, she would find him and give her thanks and expressions of everlasting affection.

Mrs Reynolds passing down the gallery beyond with a swish of skirts and jangle of keys brought Elizabeth to the entrance to the ante-room, but, as she stepped out, the door of a cabinet, an elaborate piece of furniture inlaid with oriental scenes in gold lacquer – in all probability a gift to Mr Darcy and placed in as inconspicuous a place as could be found, for he did not like the over-formal or elaborate – swung open and disgorged a load of papers on the ground at Elizabeth's feet. As it would cause more work for the servants – and Elizabeth was conscious still that her concerns in these matters would be considered laughable by great ladies such as her husband's aunt, for servants were in all respects insignificant and invisible to them – Elizabeth stooped and gathered up the letters, for such she now perceived them to be. Her surprise at first came from the freshness of the paper on which they were written; she did not think this cabinet used or visited at all. Her second sensation was one of alarm, for these were letters of a very recent nature to her husband; and, taking up the most lately written, which bore a date in October, she found herself in possession of a missive from Lady Catherine de Bourgh to her nephew, Mr Darcy. Elizabeth blushed dreadfully, and read on.

Lady Catherine presented her compliments to Mr Darcy and gave her regrets that she had perhaps been a little too outspoken on the subject of his marriage to Miss Bennet. She wished her nephew very well, and had heard from every quarter that Mrs Darcy learnt her wifely duties well and the couple gave every appearance of lasting happiness.

"But," and here Elizabeth's eyes stayed long on the page, "I must request, my dear Fitzwilliam, that you give some thought to a distant future, a future in which you will no longer be master of Pemberley. Your mother, my dear sister, spoke many times of such a time when, in the unhappy event of there being no son and heir to succeed you, the estate would pass by entail in the male line. Many times, as you may know, I tried to dissuade your father from staying with this entail – for Sir Lewis de Bourgh had no desire for an entail of such a nature at Rosings, and we are happy that our daughter shall inherit. I need not reiterate here that my grief – and I know it would have been dear Anne's too – at your decision to marry

74

Miss Bennet and not our daughter is unassuaged, and it is only to be hoped that you will not come to regret your choice.

"May I ask from you, as your aunt and sole surviving relative on your mother's side, one favour over the Christmas season? I will be brief. Your heir, Master Thomas Roper, has arrived at the age of twenty. You have not yet made his acquaintance, but I am able to give my assurance that he is a most pleasant young man, well educated, and keenly aware of his prospects, should there be no son and heir to Pemberley. I ask, simply, that I may bring Master Roper to you for Christmas. As a cousin, he may claim the right to some consideration from you; as your possible successor, he is at this time in his life in need of guidance from you – indeed, you may wish to keep him with you for a month or more, so that he may understand the principles of the management of a great estate. You may apprentice him to Mr Gresham, but I do not wish, naturally, to interfere in your affairs." The letter was ended with the usual expressions of affection and signed, with a flourish, "Your aunt Catherine de Bourgh".

Elizabeth placed the letter with the others – all, she saw, from aunt to nephew, but she had no heart to read them – and went over to stand by the window of the ante-room. Her thoughts were in turmoil: why had not Darcy told her the real relation of Master Roper to himself, for he had said only that Lady Catherine would bring her daughter; and why, when Darcy made such sport, in his new, open manner with Elizabeth, of his aunt, even going so far as to jest of a satirical playing-card of her likeness, did he fail to refuse the impertinent and premature request on the part of Lady Catherine? Why was Master Roper so freely accepted into the family?

Elizabeth, in extreme dejection, saw that, after all, Mr Darcy was little changed from his earlier self; that all her sister Jane Bingley's advice on the subject of softening him and enabling him to confide easily in his wife – advice she had taken with great earnestness – had been in vain. Darcy lived alone in his shell of Pemberley. It was his greatest concern. If his wife proved unable to present him with a son he would devote his time and tutelage, all his paternal affections very probably, to a distant cousin. Even Mr Bennet, who had, as Elizabeth had long ago accepted, many failings as a father, preferred his Elizabeth to the heir to Longbourn, Mr Collins!

From weakness, Elizabeth actually sat on a chair in the ante-room and wept half an hour. Then she made her way from the house, for the prospect of the open parkland and cold air of outdoors was necessary in the extreme to her. She did not fail to reflect, as she crossed the long galleries and descended the staircases of Pemberley, that Mrs Reynolds had suggested a bedchamber for Master Roper that had appeared at the time to Elizabeth to be stately indeed for a young bachelor cousin of the Darcy family. With the bitter sensation that everyone but she knew the true significance of the visit of Master Roper, Elizabeth left the house and made for the fields beyond the park of Pemberley.

# Seventeen

It was a fine day with a strong wind blowing, and as Elizabeth walked she reasoned with herself with a ferocity she had not known since the early days of her humiliation at the hand of Mr Darcy. Her first visit to Netherfield, the house rented by Charles Bingley – her mind returned with the speed of dream to the ball, to the haughty air of Mr Darcy, and his overheard refusal to invite Miss Elizabeth Bennet to dance, for though she was "tolerable" she was "not handsome enough" to tempt *him*. Her colour came and went as she walked over rough grass and found herself in the lane leading to the village, and she tried, by means of summoning the calm and candour of her sister Jane, to restore Mr Darcy to her favour once more. "After all," she argued, with as much determination to succeed as an attorney-at-law, "it is I, Elizabeth, who have just come from what I hoped would prove a scene of love and gratitude with my husband; I, Elizabeth, for whom Mr Darcy has constructed in his house a new library dedicated to my father – and done this for me, to show honour and respect for my forebears, even if he cannot find those sentiments for my mother. It is I, Elizabeth Darcy, who was intent on showing my respect, in turn, for the benevolence and kind paternalism of *his* late father, who was so good as to educate the scoundrel Wickham, a precedent which in no way deterred Fitzwilliam from doing likewise with young Mr Gresham. No," Elizabeth concluded, and the strength of her arguments was entirely persuasive to her, "I admire Darcy for his care of those who manage and work on his estates; and I must not refuse to grant him my appreciation of his hospitality to his cousin Master Roper. If Master Roper should one day inherit Pemberley, it is his right, and Darcy recognises it."

Elizabeth climbed a stile and entered the village. She was known and loved here now, though she had found her first visits made her awkward; for she had had no experience of the dispensing of bounty at Longbourn, Mr Bennet's estate being small, and the great houses in the vicinity seeing to it that the villagers were not neglected. Here, Elizabeth alone was responsible – and, before her coming, the wife of a retired estate manager, who was only too glad to hand over the duties to the rightful mistress of Pemberley, had officiated.

Once the first reservations had passed, Elizabeth found a delight in visiting the village and bringing her report on roofs that needed repair, or sick children, to the suitable quarters. Like all large estates, Pemberley had its own stonemason, carpenter, clockwinder and roofer; and an old nurse, once guardian of Darcy and, after him, his sister, could be called to attend to simple ailments – while the Darcy physician, at Matlock, received a regular fee from the estate in recompense for his village health visits. All in all, Pemberley, thanks to the late Mr Darcy and his son, was a model village, and Elizabeth was proud to bring some of her talents to play there. These, as she admitted when teased at her excessive modesty by her husband, were singing and dancing and a little acting (though she had no experience of the stage); and Elizabeth's pride, in her first year at Pemberley, had been the organising of the party for the children of the workers on the estate. This was to take place two days after Christmas, in the white drawing-room at Pemberley House: there would be carols, mime and a Nativity scene, all imagined by Mrs Darcy, who trained the children's voices, too, and on the discovery of an exceptionally gifted little girl had arranged harp lessons; the child's first harp performance would be heard at the party.

To be surrounded by the eager faces of the children, and to receive the smiles and curtsies of their mothers, soon rid Elizabeth of her anger and resentment – for she was now able to see it thus – at Darcy's absence of mention of Master Roper's relation to the estate. She wondered, indeed, as she entered a cottage and heard sung some verses of a favourite old hymn, at her selfishness and pride; and she prayed as earnestly as the children, in their sweet rehearsal for the big day, that she would learn to lose her propensity to prejudice.

The day had been fine, but, being at the winter solstice, turned suddenly dark – it was later than she thought – and Elizabeth, refusing an escort, announced she must hurry home. As she went down the lane and out into the fields that surrounded the park, thunder rolled in, and the first drops of stinging rain; and soon the lane turned to mud, which sucked a shoe from her foot. Thorn bushes, flailing in the gale, slapped her face.

Elizabeth stopped by an opening in the hedge and looked through at a field, still a good mile from the house, where a gypsy caravan, small and brightly painted, stood under a tree. She had passed that way several times with Georgiana, whose plaything the caravan had been; and, after a shower of icy stones had descended on her, decided to run into the field and take shelter in the caravan.

The interior was clean and bare, with only a fine carpet and some cushions, left over from the days when Georgiana had played there with her young friends; and Elizabeth sat there until the storm should pass.

As she waited, the desolation of the fading day, the increasing blackness of the sky and the dripping of the rain on the sides of the caravan inclined Elizabeth, try as she might to resist them, to fall prey to dreadful thoughts. The following day would bring all the guests to Pemberley. She would be seen in the first instance of her capacity as mistress of Pemberley; and she knew she would be judged. If arrangements failed, it was she and she only who would be to blame. However understanding Mr Darcy would prove to be – and she knew the hope was in his heart that all should go well, and mistakes would be overlooked – Elizabeth Darcy was to be responsible for both the moral and physical well-being of an ill-suited assortment of people over a long period of time. She it was who must invent diversions on dull days, provide entertainment when it was called for, whether inviting a guest to play the pianoforte and sing – and her great fear was the encouragement of her sister Mary to do either – or play commerce or fish or some new game of cards brought fresh from London by Miss Bingley and in need of mastering. Then the meals must be varied, and the platters laid out just so; and, though Elizabeth could count on Mrs Reynolds to perform her usual miracles, should some omission or fault become too evident in the arrangements, it would this year be Mrs Fitzwilliam Darcy, not the housekeeper, who must make amends.

With a succession of such musings crowding in like phantoms, Elizabeth fell into a deep sleep among the cushions of the gypsy caravan. How long she slept she did not know – she dreamed of her father, and of the library at Longbourn, where she had so often laughed and conversed with him – and she was wakened only by a beam of light from a lantern, as it shone into her face.

The light was succeeded by a voice, loud and joyful – and the face of young Mr Gresham looking down at her. He called out, "She is here, Sir. She is in here." Minutes later Mr Darcy boarded the caravan and gathered his wife up in his arms.

"My Elizabeth! What are you doing here?" he said in a voice that sounded to her exceedingly husky. "We have searched everywhere – oh God, Eliza, I thought you were lost and I would never find you again."

Dawn rose in the sky as Elizabeth returned to the house in the back of a wagon driven by Mr Gresham, with the arms of Mr Darcy around her as if he would never let her go. She was tired and stiff, and cramped; and felt more gratitude than she ever remembered, at the fine linen of her bed and the roaring fire in her room, and Darcy's arms still around her.

# Eighteen

Mrs Bennet was as astonished as she had predicted she would be by the extensiveness of the park and variety of grounds at Pemberley, and by the half-mile ascent to the top of a considerable eminence, where the wood ceased and the eye was instantly caught by the house, situated on the opposite side of a valley.

"I have never seen a place for which nature has done more," cried Mrs Bennet, who had on many occasions extracted these opinions from Mr and Mrs Gardiner, "nor a place where natural beauty has been so little counteracted by an awkward taste. To be mistress of Pemberley must be something!"

Kitty, who looked out of the window of the carriage in the hope of seeing some sign of life, though dragoons, here, would certainly be most improbable, felt her spirits go down at the sight of the handsome stone building that was Pemberley House, and remarked that the place looked as much like a prison as she had ever considered it to be.

"How can you, Kitty?" said Mrs Bennet. "You can have no idea of your good fortune, to come here as often as you do. Lady Lucas tells me she finds you much improved since the time you have spent with dear Jane at Barlow and with dear Lizzy here."

"There is nothing to do at Pemberley," was Kitty's ungracious reply.

Here Mary, who had been in silent and contemplative spirits on the journey, remarked that the library would occupy her for the length of her stay. "It is to be deplored, Kitty, that you have so little interest in the life of the intellect. Your life will be no different from Lydia's — empty and frivolous."

"I wonder, will Lydia be at Rowsley yet?" said Kitty, who was cheered by this reminder that a sister closer to her in temperament than the wise and sweet Jane, or the clever, thoughtful Lizzy, could be was to come into the vicinity. "And George Wickham," went on Kitty lazily, "I hear he has been much ill-used by Mr Darcy. What will they make of each other when they are thrown together? It is time Mr Darcy made reparation for his cruelty to brother George, that is for certain."

"My dear Kitty, you have not been listening," said Mrs Bennet. "I pray you, when tales are told, hear the other side. The truth came out that Mr Darcy was most generous to Mr Wickham."

"Lydia says her poor husband was monstrously treated," said Kitty with another yawn.

The carriage stopped in front of Pemberley House, and after Mrs Bennet had instructed Mary several times to remove her spectacles, as they gave her a slovenly air, and Kitty to shake out her dress as she alighted, so as not to appear creased after the journey, all three alighted.

"How delightful," cried Mrs Bennet, as a vista of stone bridges and a gradually rising hill, with trees scattered at just the places to charm the eye, lay before her. And "Oh, if you will pardon my daughters" – for Mrs Bennet now spoke to a footman who had opened the wide door of oak. "Let me go first! Catherine! Mary! For I am the mother of Mrs Darcy. I beg your pardon, Sir!"

This flustered beginning led to a further nervous burst of speech on Mrs Bennet's part, when, enquiring after "my daughter Mrs Darcy" and climbing the magnificent staircase to the long gallery, she was gravely informed that Mrs Darcy was still in her apartments.

"What? Still in bed? After noon?"

"Lizzy rises early, customarily," said Kitty. "Perhaps she is unwell."

"Never have I seen such stateliness," cried Mrs Bennet, as she stopped and looked around her. "My poor Elizabeth, how can she manage all this? Oh, it is very splendid indeed!"

Mrs Bennet leaned on Mary, who looked about her as if she, too, were about to faint from fear. "The rooms are so lofty and handsome! The furniture shows the fortune of the proprietor! I am quite overcome! Kitty, you never told me of the greatness of Pemberley!"

A figure could be seen to be approaching at the far end of the long gallery. As it grew nearer, Mrs Bennet and Mary, whose legs had given way beneath them, and who had lowered themselves on to a sofa, rose as best they could and assumed pleasant expressions.

"My dear Mrs Bennet," said Mr Darcy, for it was he, "please forgive my not being here to greet you on arrival." And he took the hands of Mrs Bennet and her two daughters, speaking civilly and informally to Kitty, who had already been a guest at Pemberley. "My sister looks forward to your visit," he said smiling, "and she has new songs and airs to show you."

Kitty Bennet thanked Mr Darcy for this, but without appearing excessively excited at the prospect.

"And where is my dear daughter Elizabeth?" enquired Mrs Bennet, in a tone intended to be affectionate but in fact sounding querulous, as if supposing Mr Darcy to be in charge of Bluebeard's castle, here at Pemberley.

"Elizabeth sleeps," said Mr Darcy.

"She sleeps?" cried Mrs Bennet, this time entertaining the suspicions which only her voice had betrayed earlier. "She is not well then, Mr Darcy? I must fly to her!"

Mr Darcy replied that his wife was perfectly well.

"Ah," cried Mrs Bennet, whose features became suffused with colour, "you must forgive my slowness and stupidity, my dear Mr Darcy" – and she turned and winked behind her at her daughters in a manner which even Kitty found objectionable in the extreme.

"I am told of the library at Pemberley," said Mary in a small voice, to cover the awkward silence. "Is it permissible to ask to see it?"

Mr Darcy appeared as relieved as might be expected, and insisted on conducting the party to the library instantly. "You will condone my haste, Mrs Bennet – when you have just come from a wearisome journey and would prefer to see your room . . ."

"It is a great honour to see the treasures of Pemberley in such a fashion," said Mrs Bennet hurriedly, although her feet were swelled up and painful, and her mind exclusively occupied with the condition of her daughter Elizabeth. "It is Mary who will tell you all you wish to know on the subject of books," she prattled on, as Darcy took the party to the end of the gallery and, thence, through an ante-room, to the library's new addition, still half built in walnut and elm by the estate carpenter, under the direction of Mr Gresham, who supervised, at that moment, the carving of a pediment and fluting of Grecian pillars by the workman.

Mr Darcy made introductions and Mr Gresham bowed and spoke agreeably of the plan, on being informed that his handicraft celebrated the life of the late husband of Mrs Bennet.

"I cannot see the necessity for all this!" said Mrs Bennet, who was unable to refrain from showing pique at the efforts made to order and embellish the library at Pemberley in honour of Mr Bennet rather than herself. "Mr Bennet passed many hours in the library at Longbourn, it is true, but I can wager he spent more than the half of them sitting at his table and drumming his fingers on the top!"

# Nineteen

Mrs Bennet and her daughters were shown to their rooms by the housekeeper, Mrs Reynolds, and each expressed delight at the beauties to be seen from the windows. Carriages containing the other guests could also be espied winding down the road through the park to the house, though these were then lost to sight under the portico and must needs remain a subject for conjecture until such time as the Bennets were ready to come down for dinner. An early dusk descended on the trees and wooded hills; and Mrs Bennet, when she had tired of remarking on the beauty and size of the grounds, said peevishly that she was famished, and that the dinner hour was bound to be a very great deal more advanced than at Longbourn. There, dinner was at half past three – and likely to be cleared before the cloth was laid, as Mrs Bennet surmised, at Pemberley.

Lady Catherine de Bourgh was greeted by her niece, Miss Georgiana Darcy, who must now, for all her shyness at social functions, stand in as hostess. Miss de Bourgh and Master Roper were of Lady Catherine's party; and all stood awkwardly in the hall, for Darcy had not yet made an appearance, which only served to emphasise the absence of his wife.

"Is Mrs Darcy not at Pemberley?" enquired Lady Catherine, as Master Roper eyed the approach to the long gallery keenly and expressed satisfaction at the furnishings and general splendour of the house. "I was not informed that she would be abroad at this time."

Miss Darcy replied that Elizabeth was asleep; and that she was indeed at home.

"Asleep?" said Lady Catherine in astonishment.

"Mrs Bennet and the Misses Bennet are arrived," said Miss Darcy.

"Ah, so dear Mrs Darcy entertains her family in her rooms," said Lady Catherine in a grim tone. "This is exceedingly ill-mannered."

"Perhaps, Mama, it is a long time since she has seen them," said Miss de Bourgh timidly.

"Nonsense, Anne, you have no idea of what you say," replied Lady Catherine.

Mr Darcy now appeared, and greetings took place all round. Master Roper, who was chubby and dark-haired, with a wide mouth that was none the less not good-natured, bowed low and was welcomed coolly by his host.

"Many a time have I studied the plans and architectural drawings of Pemberley, but nothing had prepared me for the felicities and magnificence," said Master Roper. "I have in my mind perfectly set out a plan of the pictures in the gallery, and I have no doubt I could place the exact spot, within an inch or two, where your latest acquisition by the late Sir Joshua Reynolds, purchased from the exhibition of his '130 performances' at the British Institution in Pall Mall, is hung. May I see if I am correct?"

"Later, Sir," said Mr Darcy in a tone now decidedly cold.

"Mrs Darcy is with her mother and sister, I am informed," said Lady Catherine. "I trust their journey was not too irksome."

"Not at all," said Mr Darcy, surprised at the misinformation. "Mrs Bennet and her daughters rest after the journey."

"And dear Mrs Darcy will be down soon?" enquired Lady Catherine de Bourgh.

Here the door opened and Miss Bingley was shown in. "I came alone, my dear Darcy," cried this young lady as she ran to the foot of the grand staircase, "for dear Charles and Jane take for ever to pack up their things and their child and their nurse and heaven knows what – and I had a carriage all to myself."

Greetings were then exchanged; and in due course Miss Bingley, who had made effusions over Miss Georgiana Darcy that brought colour to the girl's cheeks, enquired after the absent Mrs Fitzwilliam Darcy.

"Mrs Darcy is asleep, it appears," said Lady Catherine.

"Indeed!" cried Miss Bingley. "I never saw dear Mrs Darcy so ill-looking as when I was out riding in the park recently – for, as you know, Darcy, it is impossible for me to resist coming all the way from Barlow for a gallop such as yours. Dearest Eliza was quite pale in the face, I have to say, her complexion quite gone and her fine eyes dull."

Mr Darcy was about to reply to this, when he thought better of it and led his guests to the gallery.

"After dinner Anne will delight us with her new songs on the pianoforte," said Lady Catherine, on casting an eye on this instrument. "And my niece Georgiana will no doubt have added to her repertoire. Are we to assume as much from the Misses Bennet?"

Before any defence of the Bennet sisters could be put forward, however, Mrs Bennet herself appeared in the far doorway of the long gallery, her daughters on either side of her.

"I do not think, my dear Mr Darcy, that I shall ever find my way round Pemberley," cried she. "How many rooms are there, do you know?"

Mr Darcy did not reply to this, and his sister was left to perform the introductions, an office that would otherwise have been expected of his wife.

"Indeed I recall your visit to Longbourn," said Mrs Bennet to Lady Catherine de Bourgh. "You were most taken with the park, if I recall correctly."

"I have no such recollection," said Lady Catherine.

"I wager there are more rooms here than there are at Rosings," continued Mrs Bennet.

"Mama," murmured Kitty, who had been long enough in the houses of both her eldest sisters to know that this line of conversation would not be well received.

Mrs Bennet then turned to Master Roper and asked if this was his first visit to Pemberley, for an awkward silence had fallen, in which Lady Catherine declared she would go to her room before dinner, and did so.

"It is indeed, Ma'am," replied Master Roper, "though I am well acquainted with every detail of the place, from my early years. It is indeed like a dream come true."

"There will be no finer a setting for my grandson to grow up in," said Mrs Bennet in triumph. "I understand your regret, dear Master Roper, at your ineligibility for such an upbringing."

"I wish to visit the library," said Miss Mary Bennet.

Several voices were here raised, with directions on how to reach the library – for Mary, told not to wear her spectacles by Mrs Bennet, was exceedingly short-sighted and could not find her way again – and embarrassment was momentarily deflected.

"And here are Mr and Mrs Bingley," cried Miss Caroline Bingley as her brother and his wife Jane were shown in. "Why, you have taken longer in coming from Barlow than if it had been London!"

Jane Bingley did not take long to note the absence of her adored sister Elizabeth; and went on to ask Darcy if all was well with her.

"Dear Elizabeth was caught in last night's storm and drenched to the skin," replied Darcy, smiling at her sister, for she was the only one of the company to ask simply what ailed his wife. "She had perforce to shelter in a gypsy caravan in a field, and consequently she is fatigued and suffering a head-cold."

"My poor Lizzy," cried Mrs Bennet, who had heard this. "It is most inadvisable, in her condition, to go tramping the fields in a storm."

"I had no idea she went into the caravan where I used to play," said Georgiana in a childish tone.

"I used to join in your games, dear Georgiana," said Miss Bingley, "when I came to Pemberley." And here she darted a glance at Mr Darcy.

Georgiana and Miss Bingley laughed at the memory. Dinner was announced and the company proceeded to the dining-parlour.

# Twenty

Elizabeth woke and for a time had no idea of whether it was morning, eve or noon – the curtains were open, but a dark that could belong to either end of a winter's day gathered outside. If it had not been for a rustle of feet in the corridor and the sound of voices deep down in the house, she would have thought it time to sleep again, except for the absence of Darcy; and the cold bed showing he had been long gone from it.

There was a light tap at the door and Jane came in and paused, then held out her arms and went over to the invalid. "My sweetest Lizzy, are you very ill? I am so anxious for you, I had to come up."

"Oh gracious!" cried Elizabeth, struggling to sit up. "Why, they must all be here! Oh, my dear Jane, was your journey most uncomfortable, with your time so near?" And Elizabeth from weakness wept at the relief of her sister, and the fear for her, in so advanced a state of pregnancy, on the lanes from Barlow to Pemberley.

"Nonsense, Lizzy, we proceeded slowly and all was well," said the robust Jane. "And I am come to tell you that indeed they are all here, but Darcy says you are on no account to come down, he fears for *your* health, and they will all do very well without you."

"I am sure that is so," said Elizabeth with a smile, "although I know he does not mean it as it sounds. But" – and here she leaned forward and took her sister by the hand – "how does Mama fare, and Kitty and Mary?"

"They are in raptures over the board," said kind Jane, who had no wish to report Mrs Bennet's infelicities. "They are exclaiming at some of the dishes they have never before seen in their lives, and Lady Catherine even indulges them at it."

"And Miss Bingley?" enquired Elizabeth.

"Oh, she is most genial. It seems she and Miss Darcy have become the closest of friends – they plan their costume for the Pemberley ball together, in whispers."

Elizabeth rose at this and went to the cabinet to dress before Jane could arrest her in her course. "I am *not* ill, Jane," she said with a firmness her sister could only recognise and obey. "I went out last night to the village and was caught in the storm coming back. I slept a while in the caravan, that is all."

"You slept in the caravan?" cried Jane. "I am horrified, Lizzy! There are gypsies near us now, as you know, and you could have suffered terribly at their hands!"

"I have long decided to retain my freedom and walk as far afield as I please, on my own," Elizabeth replied. "I had no fear of the gypsies" – and here she came to take Jane in her arms and hold her close – "I have more to fear here at Pemberley than in the fields, dear Jane."

"I have thought of you in the last days," came Jane's soft reply. "Why do you not at least spend the remainder of the day resting – when I can see you have a cold in the head coming on?"

"I have nothing of the kind," said Elizabeth, going to the door and holding it open for her sister to pass through. "And I shall not be frightened by some of the company at Pemberley. There is a stubbornness about me that can never bear to be frightened at the actions or sayings of others. My courage always rises with every attempt to intimidate me."

So saying, Elizabeth descended the higher staircase, with Jane after her, and made her way to the dining-parlour where the company was assembled.

# Twenty-one

Elizabeth came down and into the dining-parlour, where she was warmly greeted by the assembled company. As it soon became clear that she would take neither insult nor innuendo from anyone, a silence fell as those who had been prepared to exercise their wit at her expense decided otherwise; and on those who had been about to prove too effusive, such as Mrs Bennet, the same silence descended. Master Roper alone felt at liberty to speak, and the company was entertained at length by his disquisition on the habits of various piscine varieties resident in the waters of the South Pacific.

When he at last fell silent, and had been congratulated on his far-ranging knowledge by Mr Darcy, who had none the less a smile in his eye that Elizabeth, at the far end of the table, was quick to catch, it was time to go to the long gallery and find enough amusements to fill a winter evening. Lady Catherine, whose wish it was to demonstrate the accomplishments gained by her daughter at the pianoforte in the past year, suggested that Anne should play first, and Georgiana after, to compare their prowess after so long a separation.

"I should prefer a reel," said Elizabeth, whose good humour and happiness were plain for all to see, "and I do believe Anne and Georgiana would like one too."

As both young girls smiled their evident relief at Elizabeth's light command, Miss Bingley came forward and offered to play for them. "I do not think it will last long," said she, "for Mr Darcy likes little less than to dance. Indeed, I recall at Netherfield, my dear Mrs Darcy, that he was engaged in writing a letter to his sister when the notion of a reel was put forward – as a jest, by himself – to keep us occupied and at a distance from him."

"Mr Darcy is not obliging when it comes to a reel," said Elizabeth, laughing heartily, "but he will find a way that is equally good at occupying himself, I am sure, and not deny us our amusement."

Eyes turned on Mr Darcy at this – Lady Catherine's and Mrs Bennet's most anxiously, to see how such trifling would go down; but on seeing Mr Darcy laugh as much as his wife, and to see that the master of Pemberley could now permit himself to be the subject of open pleasantry, both were surprised and once again quiet.

"Mr Darcy is much softened, Eliza!" cried Kitty, who had concealed herself on a sofa at the far end of the gallery for fear of being asked to perform, and who now came forward, hoping for a reel.

"Miss Catherine Bennet takes after her sister, Mrs Wickham," said Lady Catherine in a dry tone to Mrs Bennet. "I dare say she hopes to find dragoons in the middle of Derbyshire when the fighting is long over."

"Kitty is most interested in history," said Mrs Bennet by way of reply.

Here the music began, with Master Roper playing a fiddle to help along the reel.

"How can Master Thomas Roper find a fiddle at Pemberley?" cried Mrs Bennet. "It seems this young man can know and do anything!"

"Very true," replied Lady Catherine. "Master Roper has received the most extensive education. And he is intimately acquainted, from study of Pemberley and its geography, with the whereabouts of every room and artefact. It would have been a matter of minutes for Master Roper to locate the music-room and select an instrument. Master Roper is proficient in these things."

"I wonder why that can be," said Mrs Bennet stiffly.

The reel was well under way at this point, and Mrs Bennet's coming across the floor to put a stop to it was not taken well by the dancers.

"Why, Mama, what is the meaning of this?" cried Kitty, who was flushed with exertion and with pleasure at having just heard that there would indeed be a ball on New Year's Eve at Pemberley. "Can we not dance when we please?"

"Dear Lizzy must not fling herself about in this fashion," cried Mrs Bennet. "I am amazed that Mr Darcy will permit it."

A hush of a different sort now descended on the company, as all eyes travelled to Mr Darcy, who sat, as predicted, over a letter at a desk some way down the gallery. He did not look up at Mrs Bennet's interference.

"My daughter Mrs Darcy must take care, in her condition, to safeguard the future heir of Pemberley," Mrs Bennet expounded.

"Mama!" Jane came forward, blushing furiously. "It has been a long journey from the south of England. I beg you to retire early and not fatigue yourself further!"

Miss Bingley, rising from the piano at this, went over to Miss Georgiana Darcy and placed an arm around her shoulder. Stifled laughter could be heard as they made their way from the gallery.

"Mrs Darcy, do we have reason to expect an announcement from you?" enquired Lady Catherine, with some of the icy hauteur Elizabeth had known from her on the occasion of the great lady coming to advise the young Miss Bennet against marrying her nephew. "I have to say I was not aware of this."

"My mother confuses her two eldest daughters," said Elizabeth lightly. "As Mrs Bingley remarks, Mrs Bennet has undergone a long and fatiguing journey."

"I am come from Rosings and I am not in the slightest fatigued," said Lady Catherine de Bourgh.

The evening concluded with the drinking of tea and the performance at the pianoforte of a duet by Miss Darcy and Miss de Bourgh. Miss Mary Bennet, pressed to sing by her mother, retired instead to the library, where she was followed and lectured by Master Roper on the contents of the books on the shelves, in particular the tallest and driest tomes.

Elizabeth sat in on a game of backgammon between her husband and Charles Bingley. Lady Catherine, who sat at her embroidery, raised her head and fixed a gaze on Fitzwilliam Darcy and his young wife, from time to time.

Elizabeth, feeling the eyes of her husband's aunt were upon her, looked up and asked Lady Catherine if she would care to accompany her and her sister on a tour of the park the next day. "I think you will like the plans for the water staircases that are in progress; and Darcy has a new planting to show also, of trees so rare they must be begged from a traveller to China, or some other far-flung place!"

"I have seen enough today," said Lady de Bourgh. "On my way here I stopped to speak to the gardener: it is a habit I cannot rid myself of, for we would speak long together when Lady Anne Darcy was alive. I was horrified to see the outline of the cascades, already laid down in this park, famed for its simplicity and tranquillity."

"This is sad indeed," said Mr Darcy, smiling a little to show the extent of his grief. "Wait until you hear the water, aunt Catherine – it will soothe you, I am positive."

"Your mother detested water. I am amazed that such a desecration of her memory is permitted here. Next I will be told that a garden of stone giants – and toads – and other grotesques, such as the unwary traveller may find in Italy at the garden of Bomarzo, is intended for the park at Pemberley."

"Such a project would scarcely be necessary, Lady Catherine," said Elizabeth – who felt all her old spirit and loathing of the woman return. "For we have personages sufficiently awful here already to render the carving of such monstrosities quite superfluous."

Mr Darcy could not now mask his merriment any longer; and, after a formal exchange of wishes for a very good night, led his wife up the flight of stairs at the far end of the gallery; while Lady de Bourgh mounted the other.

# Twenty-two

Jane Bingley's advanced pregnancy led her to accept an invitation to lie abed in the morning; and to her bedchamber Elizabeth came, when she had conferred with Mrs Reynolds on the fare of the day.

"I do not believe it can be borne!" cried Elizabeth. "Mama worse than even my nightmares told; and so many days and weeks of it to come!"

"Hush, dear Lizzy. Mama will be calm soon. It has been too much of an excitement for her, to come here to Pemberley, where she has never been before, and to see you when such a time has gone by," said Jane. "She will soon occupy herself with Lydia and her children, when they visit; and she will be invited by kind aunt Gardiner to Rowsley, I have no doubt of it."

"Oh Jane, I am not what I should be!" said Elizabeth, whose eyes filled with tears. "I could not bring myself to ask our mother to visit here for so long – and when I do, I cannot wait for her to leave! How can you bear that she will be in the vicinity when your child is born, poking her way into your house at Barlow, into the home where you are so happy with Charles, as I was happy here at Pemberley!"

"You *are* happy here at Pemberley with Darcy," said Jane quietly, for she knew Elizabeth's impulsive nature, as quickly gay as sad. "And for us, you know, the child brings all the compensation that could ever be asked for. Mama's ways will go unheeded, when it comes to it."

"Ah," said Elizabeth, hanging her head. "I do not know the happiness you speak of, Jane – but how I do yearn for it! I am not good enough for Darcy as I am, you know – he *must* wonder that I cannot give him a child – and his two previous brides, as they were intended to be, Miss Caroline Bingley and Miss de Bourgh, here at Pemberley and recalling to him that he might have a thriving family here by now!"

"But Darcy loves *you*, Eliza," said Jane, "and he will wait patiently, you will see. I'll wager there's a child here next Christmas, and all this will be forgotten!"

Elizabeth kissed her sister. "I most fervently hope so, my sweet Jane. And now you must think of yourself and not of me, for I am such a selfish creature!"

"You are the bravest creature I have ever known," cried Jane, "for there are few who could bear such a gathering as we have here at Pemberley."

"Without mention of Master Thomas Roper!" said Elizabeth, and both sisters laughed heartily.

# Twenty-three

The morning was occupied, for Elizabeth, by conducting her mother and Mary about the grounds at Pemberley; and, before they had reached the area of the garden where water staircases were to be constructed, Mr Darcy joined the party with a group that consisted of his aunt, Lady Catherine, his sister, and Miss Bingley.

"Your cascades will be all very fine," said Mrs Bennet to Elizabeth, "but I have so much to hear from you, my dear Lizzy, and so much to tell! Can we not go somewhere more enclosed, I do beg you! To come so far – and to find we are like strangers, Lizzy!"

Elizabeth was about to comply with this request – though as unwilling as it was possible to be – when a phaeton with four ponies was espied on the road at the highest point of the park and directly facing the house. A cheer emanated from the vehicle, as it approached; and Lady de Bourgh turned to her nephew in some consternation.

"And who are these, Darcy? Is it deemed correct, in this age, at Pemberley, for any person to make a trip here who pleases?"

Master Thomas Roper, who had been searching eagerly for the party, came along the path at this moment and gave his audience the benefit of his knowledge on the subject.

"There will be a hyper-quantity of visitors such as this by the next century," said Master Roper. " 'Trippers', indeed – from the towns such as Manchester, whose insalubrious air will drive its citizens out to the freshness and peace of a place such as Pemberley."

"And you would admit them all?" cried Lady Catherine.

"It would be anti-charitable indeed, not to," said Master Roper, "for we are about to witness a great increase in the population; and if one tourist is permitted to apply here, to see the beauties of Pemberley and take the air, then I can see only pseudo-reasons why a great mass of people should not come."

"Mr Darcy will not approve of this," said Lady Catherine, who now appeared most displeased at the notion of the park crowded with the uninvited and the ill-bred – "do you, Darcy?"

Mr Darcy, however, did not reply to his aunt – and came across the grass to take Elizabeth's arm. "And what do you think of the subject of Pemberley open to a mass of people?" he asked gently; but Elizabeth could see that he smiled in reality at the assumptions of Master Roper and Lady Catherine. "Would you make a toll-gate? Let them through when they pleased? I suspect the latter, if I know my wife."

"Here is the test of it," said Miss Bingley, who was more and more put out by the happiness and contentment to be found at Pemberley. "Let us see what Mrs Darcy will decide with these visitors – do they trespass, or do they not?"

The phaeton, as it descended the hill opposite and rattled across the bridge, could now be seen to be carrying at least seven people – of which three, very young children, gave the cheers heard echoing across the hills.

"Why, it is my dear sister Gardiner," cried Mrs Bennet, as she peered distractedly at the approaching party. "And Lydia and my son-in-law Wickham and their dear children – bless me if it is not!"

"They are not the kind of people one would expect to find at Pemberley," said Lady Catherine to Miss Bingley. "I suppose they come from Manchester, or some such place."

Mr Gardiner was also of the party; and he disembarked holding a fishing-rod.

"What can Darcy be thinking of?" Miss Bingley said. "This is not a season for salmon. He cannot have encouraged this . . . gentleman . . . to bring tackle with him to Pemberley!"

"My uncle Mr Gardiner is a dedicated angler," said

Elizabeth, for she had heard this. "He will be satisfied with a little coarse fishing."

"I dare say," was Lady Catherine's reply.

Elizabeth had little time to ponder the rudeness of her husband's aunt – or to stop and hear from Master Roper of the many categories of fish, from chubb to grayling to roach, that Mr Gardiner might be expected to find at the end of his line – for she understood now that it was Darcy, and none other, who had sent for her relatives from Rowsley in this way. Had not Mrs Gardiner exclaimed, on her first visit to Pemberley, that she would take the greatest pleasure in going round the park in a phaeton and ponies? Had not Darcy decided, as another expression of his boundless esteem and affection for his wife, to surprise her yet again with a gesture at once generous and thoughtful? It was as much as Elizabeth could do to refrain from running to him then and there and throwing herself in his arms. She did not – but she could see Darcy note her heightened colour and shining eyes – and she received pleasure from him once more in return when, on effecting the introduction of his in-laws, he made reference to the fact that it was he who had sent for them with a phaeton from the stables at Pemberley.

Elizabeth recalled the feelings of regret she had known on first coming to Pemberley, having refused Darcy and now half in love with him, that she would never know the pleasures of being mistress of such a place; and the relief which had succeeded the regret, when she considered that her dear aunt and uncle Gardiner would not be invited to visit, should she be Mrs Darcy, thus ruling out too much wistfulness at the lost prospect. And here were Mr and Mrs Gardiner – in full view of Lady Catherine de Bourgh and Miss Bingley! Elizabeth had not known such delicacy before in a man, as was shown by Mr Darcy, and in her mind she thanked God for him very sincerely.

George Wickham's arrival inspired little joy in the party, however; and Elizabeth was soon aware that it was she, as hostess and as relative of the contingent from Rowsley, who must repay Darcy's noble gesture with tact and discretion on

her own part. There was Miss Georgiana Darcy to consider –
for, on seeing the man who had abducted her and carried her
off to Ramsgate but a few years before, she went exceedingly
pale and clung to Miss Bingley. There was Darcy himself –
who, as she well knew, had saved her sister Lydia's reputation
when the scoundrel Wickham had eloped with her, and, due
to the smallness of her fortune, in all probability without
the slightest intention of marriage. Darcy, who had bribed
Wickham to make an honest woman of Lydia! When he had
suffered already the dishonesty of the young protégé of his late
father; and had heard the lies and libels about himself so freely
spread by Wickham. It was a kind gesture indeed, to send a
phaeton that would include George Wickham as a passenger,
to return to the place he had robbed and betrayed.

"It is most pleasant to be at Pemberley again," said
Wickham, who appeared unaware of the turmoil his arrival
must occasion. "I see the oaks planted in the park are a very
great deal taller, Darcy!"

Mrs Bennet cut short the possibility of a reply to this
from Mr Darcy – should one have been forthcoming – by
greeting Lydia and her children with all the effusiveness of
a grandmother long denied access to her loved ones. She
remarked again and again that the children had grown faster
than the trees; and, on the arrival in the Long Walk of little
Emily Bingley with her father, insisted on taking the children to
the bridge, to measure their heights against the stone parapet.
"Jane, Lizzy, come here! Do you see how Lydia's second son
resembles dear Lizzy? Lydia, I swear he is the image of her and
this must come through me, for Mr Bennet had a head that
was quite disagreeably square!"

"I will be happy to oblige with some recent findings on
phrenology," said Master Roper, coming over to the bridge
where they stood. "It is a proven fact that a murderer will have
a bump here – and here" – and Master Roper demonstrated his
theory on the head of young Toby Wickham, who promptly
started to cry – "and his ear-lobes will also be preternaturally
small!"

Lady Catherine here declared her intention of walking down

to the bower, by the stream; and she took Miss Darcy and Miss Bingley with her. They passed close enough to Elizabeth, whether by design or by accident, for her to hear their conversation – which went as follows:

"I do not believe Darcy will tolerate these screaming children at Pemberley, do you, my dear Miss Bingley?"

"Indeed, I do not. For I know as well as you do, Lady Catherine, that Darcy detests children. He has spoken to me often of a total absence of any desire to bring a child into the world."

"And to me, also," said Lady Catherine, as the party passed down to the water's edge. "I have to say that my plans for Anne were much dictated by this knowledge. For Anne has Rosings to hand down directly, as you know, Miss Bingley, and for her to have married a man not in the least philoprogenitive might almost certainly have proved most undesirable!"

Elizabeth stood a moment between the bridge and the water after hearing this. Her first instinct was to burst out laughing; her next to run to Darcy and claim from him an immediate rebuttal of the ridiculous claims of Lady Catherine and Miss Bingley. For did not Darcy give time and thought – when it was available to him – to the children of his estate workers, did he not lift little Emily Bingley high in the air, only this morning, when she came down the path with her hoop, led by her devoted father?

Mr Darcy, Elizabeth noted with a sense of dread, had been caught by Mrs Bennet and was as pinioned by her against the parapet of the bridge as the Wickham children – for Mrs Bennet came ever closer to him, and poor Mr Darcy was in danger of slipping into the water altogether.

"I was saying," cried Mrs Bennet, who had one arm round Lydia and the other brandishing wildly, as she drew on family resemblances, "I was saying, my dear Lizzy, that little Toby does not only take after you! No, he has a distinct look of Mr Darcy as well – I cannot think how that can be!"

"Madam!" said Mr Darcy – and Elizabeth saw he looked most displeased; she had come too late to stop the foolishness of her mother. "If you will permit me, I have business which awaits with my steward."

So saying, Mr Darcy strode off; and from his pace and lowered head Elizabeth knew there was no catching him.

"Mama, why do you talk so?" And to Lydia, who wore a fatuous smile at the supposition voiced by her mother of her son's taking after the great Mr Darcy, Elizabeth spoke harshly: "*Why* do you permit Mama to say these things? They are not agreeable to Mr Darcy, I assure you!"

"My dear Lizzy, we think only of your future happiness," said the fatuous Mrs Bennet. "We wish to remind Mr Darcy of his duties as a husband and a father."

Elizabeth's horror grew at this; and, seeing Mrs Reynolds come down from the house towards her, she went quickly up the bank to meet her.

Mrs Reynolds said that a gentleman had come to Pemberley; said he was invited; and waited in the hall with John.

"I have invited no one," said Elizabeth. Then, recalling that the Mayor of Barlow had on her last visit to Jane offered contributions for the purchase of musical instruments for the children of the estate workers, to be presented at the party at Pemberley, she related this to Mrs Reynolds and asked her if this could be the visitor.

"No, he is not the Mayor," said Mrs Reynolds. "And if it had been, Madam, I would have given him the news that there is now to be no party for the children here."

"What?" cried Elizabeth.

"The party will not take place," said Mrs Reynolds, who now looked at Elizabeth askance. "So I am informed by Mr Darcy, as he came from the steward's house just five minutes ago."

Elizabeth hid her anger; and, on seeing John the footman come out on to the south front, went up to him and asked if the visitor who waited in the hall had given a name.

John replied that the mysterious caller had "wished to surprise" the party at first, but had now vouchsafed his name and the lady on whom he particularly called.

"A Colonel Kitchiner to see Mrs Bennet, Madam," said John.

# Twenty-four

Jane Bingley was at the head of the grand staircase by the west entrance to Pemberley House when her mother, agitated in the extreme, came in from the south front and saw her there.

"Where is he?" cried Mrs Bennet, for the hall was empty of people. "Where is Colonel Kitchiner?"

"He has been assisted to Mrs Reynolds's sitting-room," said Jane. "And now, Mama, pray tell us who Colonel Kitchiner may be."

"Mrs Reynolds's sitting-room?" said Mrs Bennet in a desperate tone. "Pray – it is your turn to explain why he was shown *there*? It is an insult from which he will not quickly recover."

"Whether that be so or not," said Jane, "Colonel Kitchiner mistook me for the lady of the house. He went so far as to compliment me on being about to bring forth a son and heir to Pemberley. He then feigned knowledge of me, and of my husband; and spoke of Lydia too. You will do me the honour of saying, before poor Lizzy has the impostor thrown out, what are the credentials that bring this visitor here?"

Elizabeth came into the hall at this moment. She had made enquiries of Mrs Reynolds and wanted only corroboration from Jane that some mistake had happened, and a stranger admitted to Pemberley without good reason, to order his immediate eviction from the house.

"My dear Lizzy," cried Mrs Bennet, "I have not had time to tell you all that has befallen me since I last wrote. Oh, I did beg that we might go to some quiet place in the park together, but so much happened all at once!"

"How does this visitor know so much of your daughters

103

and their families?" demanded Jane; and seeing that Elizabeth looked very white in the face – though from what other causes she could not know – she assumed that the incident upset her sister, and came down to ask her mother to clear up the mystery quickly, for there were many other responsibilities which Elizabeth must shoulder, in the managing of a house such as Pemberley.

"My dear Jane," cried Mrs Bennet, for she did not know which daughter to turn to, "I fear the colonel has been a little precipitate in coming here so early in the season. But this must bode well for all of us – for it must show he has a fervour which cannot be restrained, that his love burns as bright as it did all of thirty years ago in Meryton."

"Mama," said Elizabeth, who was now thoroughly alarmed, "are you perfectly well? To what do you refer? We never heard tell of a Colonel Kitchiner – neither Jane nor I. It is certain."

"You were not born," said Mrs Bennet. "He is a cousin, dear Lizzy and Jane – his father was a solicitor, my father's partner in Meryton – and you have shown him to the housekeeper's room! How am I treated in my own daughter's house!"

"No, no, Mama," Jane said, "Mrs Reynolds was good enough to explain that her sitting-room is on the ground floor, at the back – and then it took such a time for John to find you."

"What if it is on the ground floor?" sobbed Mrs Bennet. "Colonel Kitchiner has asked me to be his wife! He leaves all he has, in his will, to poor Kitty and Mary, including a marvellous pleasant house at Lyme with a sea view and a porch. I am horrified at the way he has been treated. I must report directly to Mr Darcy on this!"

Jane and Elizabeth stood a moment quite still, as they received this latest information from Mrs Bennet. Then, as Jane began to speak to her mother, a tapping was heard on the flagstones of the passage which led away from the hall to the servants' quarters.

"Colonel Kitchiner was shown the ground-floor sitting-room on account of his wooden leg," said Jane, as the man himself opened the door into the hall and entered. "I am positive that no offence was intended or taken, Mama."

Mrs Bennet's gasp, whether of horror or of disbelief, was muted by the descent, from the great staircase, of Master Thomas Roper – and by the time Elizabeth, who appeared also to be too shocked to speak, had made herself known to the new visitor, all expressions of astonishment had passed, and Mrs Bennet was able to cross the hall very nearly in command of herself.

"May I enquire, Sir, as to where you lost your limb?" said Master Roper, before Mrs Bennet and her old friend could greet each other. "For I can see that it was not at Waterloo!"

"Excuse me, Sir?" said Colonel Kitchiner.

"I'll wager it was at Amiens, for it is replaced finely, and the best surgeons are from that part of France," said Master Roper gravely.

Elizabeth, at this, fled from the hall by the door to the west front, and ran – she cared not where. She carried with her the very red face of Colonel Kitchiner, and a sight of bulbous jowls, all of which seemed to contradict each other as he spoke; and wispy white hair on a mottled bald pate. As she ran she prayed to find Darcy and be comforted by him at this latest folly on the part of Mrs Bennet – until she recalled that she needed first a most cogent explanation from him: the party on which she had toiled and planned for so many months, cancelled without reference to her? The children to be let down with so much anticipation built up in them? He must supply a very good reason for this.

Elizabeth reflected, as she went searching for Darcy at the steward's house, that only the appearance of a prospective stepfather such as Colonel Kitchiner could have banished a topic of such gravity from her mind. And it was not long before she thought of Mr Bennet, and his very likely remarks on her mother's suitor – and she wept a little, as she went through the rough grass to find her husband.

# Twenty-five

Mr Gresham's house – for, as steward of the Pemberley estates, the senior Mr Gresham had a life tenancy there – lay on the outskirts of the village, but still within the confines of the park; and Elizabeth hastened her step, as a light rain came on and there were signs of more to come in the dark clouds in the sky.

She could not refrain, as she approached the neat, pleasant house, from reflecting on the last tenant there, Mr Wickham; and the son to whom so much had been promised, and who had disappointed so many, with his dishonesty and deceit; nor could she keep herself from sighing at the thought of poor Lydia tied to a man so little able to provide for a family and so lacking in feeling for her. Then it was but a moment before gratitude to Darcy – who received Wickham at Pemberley, who must support him after all as a brother-in-law! – recalled to Elizabeth her very real obligations to her husband. Wickham might not be a guest in the house, but he would eat dinner with them today – it was dreadful – and now, to compound the horrors, there was Colonel Kitchiner to see. She decided, as she went to the door of the steward's house, that she must ask without ill humour of the future of the children's party at Pemberley; that she was beholden to Darcy as never before; and that it was her place to cajole him back to the smiles and witticisms they had both so much enjoyed, rather than the other way around. When she considered, too, the sentiments which must be his when Master Roper strutted in the house and grounds; and how near he must come to yearning for some glad tidings from Elizabeth, that a child would be born to them and Master Roper banished for ever, she found herself on the point of making a decision not to raise the subject of the village children at all. How Darcy must loathe and detest this bees' nest that was the house party at Pemberley! – the scorn of his aunt coming out despite herself; the silliness of Mrs Bennet and Kitty; the sharp tongue of Miss Bingley! In her understanding of the absent Mr Darcy, Elizabeth quite forgot her own feelings; or, rather, forgot to see that they were hers and that she imputed them also to him.

For when the door was opened, the young Mr Gresham stood there and gave a very different reason for Darcy's distracted air and sudden departure from the family party by the river at Pemberley.

"Mr Darcy is gone to Matlock," said Mr Gresham, "and my father is gone with him." Then – seeing Elizabeth had rain on her hair and shawl – "But will you not come in and dry by the fire? You should not get wet again, after the episode in the caravan."

Young Mr Gresham was so easy a companion – he was about her own age, Elizabeth thought, and with pleasant features, a fresh complexion and light-brown hair – that she had no difficulty in accepting the invitation. Mrs Gresham, his mother, soon came through from the parlour, and gave Elizabeth a chair by the fire, and offered a dish of tea, which was warmly accepted.

Elizabeth had not at first wished to show that she had no knowledge of Mr Darcy's intended departure for Matlock; but the Greshams were so agreeable, and the fire so warm, that she resolved to ask them also if they knew the reason for stopping the children's party at this late hour.

"Why, Mr Darcy had no notion of going to Matlock, until he came over here and we told him the news," said old Mrs Gresham. "The parson there had a fall, and died; Mr Darcy has the patronage of the church there, and had to go, to visit the widow."

Ah, I see, thought Elizabeth; so his going does not account for his temper when he left us – it is all my mother's doing;

and she wished intensely for her sister Jane, to relieve her of her bitterness.

"He will stay the night, he told us," said Mrs Gresham, who now looked uncomfortable on seeing the stricken expression on Elizabeth's face, "because it will come on to rain, and there is no more desolate road at this time of year," the good woman added hastily.

Mr Gresham here started to tell Elizabeth the plans for the new wing of the library at Pemberley; this he did in the gentlest and most engaging manner possible, and soon Elizabeth had only fond memories of her father's bookish habits to pass on to Mr Gresham – for he had been permitted entry since an early age, and knew every book there.

"The new catalogue is indeed important," said he, as Elizabeth rose to take her leave. "I believe Mr Darcy's young cousin Master Roper found the present arrangement most confusing."

"Was he disagreeable to you?" asked Elizabeth sharply; for she saw that Mr Gresham looked away when he spoke. But "Master Roper is perhaps not as knowledgeable as he assumes in certain areas" was all she could get out of Mr Gresham. And, as Elizabeth made her way across the room, the young librarian and his mother accompanied her to the door of the steward's house.

"It has stopped raining," said Mr Gresham, "or I would go to the village and fit up a pony and trap for you, Mrs Darcy."

Elizabeth replied that she had a mind to go to the village herself. "The children looked forward to a party with carols and entertainments at Pemberley. Can you have any notion why this will now not take place?" she said. "I understand there must be a good reason – but we were so many, out taking a walk in the park, that I did not have time to discover – " Seeing this sounded lame, Elizabeth broke off.

Mr Gresham, with his mother behind him on the doorstep, appeared so concerned by her words that he was silent – but whether another instance of the lack of communication between Mr Darcy and his wife had shocked him into a loss

108

of speech could not be ascertained, for Mrs Gresham stepped forward at this point and said with emphasis that they had heard nothing of this at the steward's house.

"And that is why I thought he had come here, for Mrs Reynolds said she heard it from him as he left this house," cried poor Elizabeth, who now knew herself to be less a confidante of Mr Darcy than a servant. "I am mistaken, perhaps – or Mrs Reynolds mistook the import of Mr Darcy's remarks. I will go directly to the village – they will tell me there!"

Both Mr Gresham and his mother came out of the house and, with voices raised, implored Elizabeth to return home; and not to take the road to the village. "Look at those rain clouds," said Mr Gresham. "I shall certainly fetch you a pony and trap, Mrs Darcy, if you do not hasten back now."

"There will be a party out looking for you again," said Mrs Gresham. "It is for your own health and welfare that you return to Pemberley House."

Elizabeth promised she would; and she set off obediently enough down the lane. Once the figures of Mrs Gresham and her son had gone inside and the door closed, however, she turned and, taking a short-cut across a field behind the steward's house, soon found herself by the first cluster of cottages in the village.

She made her way over the puddles that had increased in size since the storms of two nights ago; and turned down by the forge, in search of the blacksmith's wife, who had been a helper and guide with the planning of the children's entertainment at Pemberley. A light rain started to fall again; and she pulled her shawl over her head. A mass of loose stones in the middle of the thoroughfare caused her to stumble, and lay her hand for support on the wattle wall of the blacksmith's cottage – and it was then, as she righted herself, and received a curious glance from a passing villager – for surely this was not the mistress of Pemberley, in this rain and on a gloomy day such as this – that she saw Mr Darcy stride out of a house at the end of the street, with a boy of about six years old at his side.

Mr Darcy and his young companion crossed the street and turned up by the church – and, as Elizabeth ran after them and called Darcy's name, they turned again into a cobbled alley where the houses were of extreme antiquity, and went through an entrance to one of them – the building in such decay that the door swung open on its hinges – and disappeared.

At first Elizabeth thought she must have dreamed the entire episode. The light was dim; the rain was falling now steadily; and it was possible – was it possible? – that a man of the height and presence of Darcy had stopped in the village, in need of the blacksmith – but then, where was his horse? And, if there was no horse, why was Darcy on foot, when he was supposed to have gone to Matlock? Certainly he would have gone that distance on horseback. If he was not in Matlock, what was he doing here?

Elizabeth's thoughts were in turmoil, and she felt her colour come and go and her breathing grow harsh and short. Had Mr Gresham and his mother purposely misled her, when they told of her husband's mission of mercy to the widow of an incumbent parson? Was there a good reason for them to try all they could do to dissuade her from visiting the village? She could barely bring herself to consider the implications of this – for, if Darcy had a secret from her, all the love and trust built up and maintained since their marriage would be nothing. And this could not be true. So Elizabeth's thoughts went wildly, until she saw, on retracing her steps to the forge – for an exploration of the ancient alley had shown only that the houses there acted as mere conduits to the lane on the far side – that there was a pony and trap, with Mr Gresham in the driver's seat, waiting in the small square at the head of the lane.

Elizabeth was torn between anger and relief on perceiving this. Had Mr Gresham followed her, then? Did she have no freedom, no independence of movement, as the mistress of Pemberley? Must the son of the steward be appointed steward of the wife of Mr Darcy, as his father managed the land? She turned, with a sudden idea to go through the abandoned houses and play hide-and-seek with her pursuer – when

110

Mr Gresham, alighting from the pony and trap, came down the lane and civilly enquired whether he could offer Mrs Darcy a ride back to the house. As, by now, several pairs of eyes were trained on the bedraggled Mrs Darcy – and tongues wagged that this was the second time in as many days that she was seen here, getting a soaking – Elizabeth could do no other than accept Mr Gresham's offer with a good grace.

The drive back to Pemberley took place without a word exchanged between Elizabeth and Mr Gresham. If she wished to enquire further as to the whereabouts of Mr Darcy – or, this pushed once more into the background by dramatic events, demand a reason for the cursory arrest of the children's party – Elizabeth found she could not do so. She did not know where she could place her trust, now; she needed her sister Mrs Bingley's calmness and counsel; and she prayed that Mrs Bennet would be satisfactorily engaged elsewhere, when she came back into the house.

Elizabeth's prayer was not to be answered. After thanking Mr Gresham in a manner that showed her dislike of being followed, and over-protected – a stiff expression of thanks which provoked in Mr Gresham a wounded and startled look – she went into the west entrance and found her mother in the hall, in a state of great agitation.

"Thank the Lord, Lizzy – you are here! I have told Mrs Reynolds I would watch for you, as she awaits the doctor and gives orders to the servants – "

"The doctor?" said Elizabeth, whose blood ran cold at the thought that Darcy had fallen from his horse – that he was dead – that she had seen his phantom in the village, just half an hour before.

"Jane is started on her confinement!" cried Mrs Bennet. "The doctor from Barlow has been sent for, but the rain makes the road so bad . . ." Here Mrs Bennet broke down and wept; and Elizabeth went to comfort her as best she could.

"Hush, Mama! I am certain there is no need for you to wait down here – come upstairs and be more comfortable – where is John?"

"John is called to the cellar by Master Roper," replied

111

Mrs Bennet distractedly. "And I wish to accompany the medical man myself to the bedside of poor Jane!"

"I shall go to her immediately," said Elizabeth, and she went to the stairs and began to go up. "Why does Master Roger instruct John to visit the cellar?" she now said, as the notion appeared to her very odd.

"Mr Darcy is away at Matlock," said Mrs Bennet, who peered up at Elizabeth, and spoke through her tears. "So Master Roper chooses the wines for dinner, Lizzy."

Does he indeed? thought Elizabeth – but she would not permit herself to be distracted, and ran on up the stairs to reach her sister Jane.

"He has been kind enough to extend an invitation to dinner to Colonel Kitchiner," Mrs Bennet called after her; "and he chooses the port, also, and some fine liqueur brandies, for we are, after all, dear Lizzy, arrived at the eve before Christmas."

These last words were lost on Elizabeth, as she went the length of the long gallery and found the stairs to the floor where Jane's bedchamber lay.

# Part Three

# Twenty-six

Dinner at Pemberley in Mr Darcy's absence was a flustered affair. Elizabeth was downstairs late a second time, after her visit to Mrs Bingley, and a wait for the medical man, a Dr Mason from Barlow who came with difficulty through snow, in the dark of the closing of a winter's day. Mrs Bennet came and went throughout the meal, complaining of her nerves as much as expressing anxiety over her daughter. And the servants, hoping for direction from the mistress of the house, found themselves, as a consequence of Mrs Darcy's not unreasonable distraction, given orders by Master Roper, who had placed himself at the head of the table.

Elizabeth knew this was grotesque – but there was little she could do to change the situation; and what gave her, probably, more annoyance than the posturings of Darcy's cousin was the clear expression of pleasure and satisfaction at this placement to be found on the face of Miss Bingley. It was mortifying, also, to see Miss Georgiana Darcy giggle with Miss Bingley and cast looks that were not all friendly at Elizabeth – it would only be concluded that the girl had fallen under the influence of a young woman both older and more accomplished than herself and that she would soon regret it – but, for the present, the camaraderie of Caroline Bingley and Georgiana was provocative to her in the extreme.

If only Jane were here – if only Jane could be confided in now! – for, on looking round the table, Elizabeth could swear there was no one she could feel for, no one she could tell of the strange vision of Mr Darcy and the child in the village today; no one of whom she could ask simple advice. Indeed, it appeared to her that she was surrounded more by

enemies than by friends. Master Roper, who had seated Lady
Catherine on his right hand, looked down the table at her
with what she saw as an air of evil complacency; George
Wickham – with whom once she had fancied herself almost
in love, before she knew him for the fortune hunter and rascal
that he was – ogled Miss Darcy across the table and gave
no attention to the desperate attempts on the part of Lydia
to claim his conjugal attentions; and Colonel Kitchiner, who
sat by Mrs Bennet when she was *in situ*, huffed and puffed in
a manner so obsequious and false that Elizabeth knew there
could never be any serious colloquy with him. Only aunt and
uncle Gardiner, in their innocence and kindness unaware of
the impudence of Master Roper at claiming Mr Darcy's chair
as his own, bore all the affection for Elizabeth which any
hostess of a large family gathering might hope to expect. But
how could she confide her doubts to *them* – of all people
the most certain, after initial wonderment at the grandeur
of Elizabeth's match, that she had done the right thing?
– to reveal to *them* that she knew little of her husband's
movements; that she did not know, even, that Mr Darcy
was really gone to Matlock to see about the living become
vacant there? No, the Gardiners, who spoke now of the
snow gathering outside and of the urgent necessity to return
to Rowsley before they were unable to use the roads, must
consider the marriage of their dear niece and Mr Darcy as
sacrosanct.

"My dear lady," Elizabeth now heard Colonel Kitchiner
address Mr Darcy's aunt, "I am most intrigued by your
method of eating a pear! So exquisite a slicing method; such
delicacy of poise on the fork of purest mother-of-pearl!"

"I had hoped for some fishing tomorrow," said Mr
Gardiner, as Elizabeth wished herself at the bottom of the sea
and Lady Catherine munched on, regardless, "for Mr Darcy
was good enough to invite me to come again to Pemberley and
try my line where the stream runs deepest – indeed, it is like a
little glen down that part of the park, is it not?"

"I do not find any resemblance with Scotland," said Lady
Catherine de Bourgh.

"The fall of snow is not so dissimilar," said Mrs Gardiner with a smile.

Mrs Bennet, who had been out of the room for a time, here bustled in.

"How is dear Jane?" cried Lydia and Kitty, who sat together, discussing their costumes for the Pemberley New Year's Ball in low tones. "Is she delivered yet?"

"I have never known such topics discussed downstairs," said Lady Catherine, and she and Miss Bingley exchanged glances. Elizabeth did not miss this, and she suggested that the carriage be prepared for Mr and Mrs Gardiner's party – "and, Kitty, you will perhaps like to go to Rowsley for the night," she added, for Kitty, once so improved with her long visits to her two eldest sisters, seemed to have descended, after so short a time in the company of her mother and sister, to the level from which Elizabeth had so dearly hoped her rescued.

"Oh, I should be happy to do that!" cried Kitty. "But what of sister Jane? Will she not be in need of us tonight?"

"She will do well without you," said Elizabeth; and she made to rise from the table, to lead the ladies to the boudoir.

"I am certain it will be tonight, though Dr Mason fears it may be a breech birth," said Mrs Bennet, who showed no sign of understanding Elizabeth's discomfiture. "And I am certain it will be a boy – " Here she broke off, looked around the table, and dropped her voice. "There is a sure way of procuring a boy . . ." Here she confided in Mrs Gardiner, who, good-natured though she was, flinched from Mrs Bennet's confidences on the subject.

"This is not to be endured," said Lady Catherine, rising and leading the way from the dining-room without waiting for the hostess to do so.

"And what might the method be, of procuring a boy?" said Miss Bingley, who now enjoyed herself hugely and encouraged Miss Darcy to do likewise.

"Why, it comes from a Frenchwoman I once had the acquaintance of," said Mrs Bennet. "They are more advanced than we are in such matters, you know."

"I believe there is proof of this," said Miss Bingley gravely.

Master Roper, with some ostentation, here lifted the decanter of port, as a signal for the ladies to depart from the dining-parlour. "You will be interested to learn," said Master Roper to Colonel Kitchiner, "that there is little that I do not know on the subject of musketry – of all military manoeuvres in the Napoleonic Wars. Indeed I consider myself a connoisseur and look forward to discussing the campaigns in which you had the honour to serve, Sir."

"Do you, Sir?" said Colonel Kitchiner, who was now of a deeper hue than the port; and snuffling and huffing as if pursued by huntsmen. "I am obliged to you, Sir – but I must . . ." – and Colonel Kitchiner made to rise from the table, this being accomplished with difficulty, for the wine he had drunk and the awkward placing of his artificial limb all stood in the way of success.

Elizabeth went to take the arm of her aunt Gardiner, and led the remainder of the ladies from the room; for Miss Anne de Bourgh, who had been as sickly and silent as ever all through dinner, had gone through with her mother, for coffee. As they went, their progress was impeded by an attempt on the part of Colonel Kitchiner to leave the room, likewise.

"No, pray stay here, my dear Colonel," cried Master Roper, who now strode to the side-table before the ladies had properly left the room, and extricated a chamberpot from the cupboard below. "Those wounded fighting for the Crown may at least count on this as comfort – I am sure there are many households, some of the best in the land, who still provide such facilities – and if it were not for the new mode of sensibility prevalent in the country, the habit would go unchanged."

Colonel Kitchiner was left speechless by Master Roper's offer. Elizabeth closed the door of the dining-parlour behind her too late, as she knew, for Miss Bingley and Georgiana were now convulsed. As she led her aunt to the room where coffee awaited, she felt her own colour rise and fall, and was aware Mrs Gardiner saw it.

Elizabeth's thoughts were so filled with anger that she must needs recall the pain and struggle at this very moment suffered upstairs by her dear sister Jane, and she determined to go straight to her, when Mrs Gardiner was settled. But for now – "how dare Master Roper commit such vulgarity in my home?" – and here Elizabeth saw herself for the first time truly the mistress of Pemberley, just when she doubted Mr Darcy and thus her own future happiness there. "How can it be permitted that this odious young man takes on the mantle of Mr Darcy; even goes so far as to invite a man so dreadful as Colonel Kitchiner, who, for all we know, sees Mrs Bennet as a rich widow and comes to her for her fortune, out of nowhere? And Georgiana! What has come over her?"

These thoughts of Elizabeth's, which resembled the wild flurries of snow falling outside – for they raced and whirled and could not come together with any calmness – were put to an end by her mother's arrival in the boudoir, where Lady Catherine and her daughter took coffee.

"The gentlemen are at their port," cried Mrs Bennet on espying the two ladies sitting quietly, "and my daughter awaits me upstairs. Can your ladyship be kind enough to pardon me if I go up to her directly?"

Elizabeth was now the subject of conflicting emotions, for her desire to remove her mother from the company of Lady Catherine was matched by the desire to save her poor sister from Mrs Bennet's attentions in childbirth. She paused a moment, therefore – which Miss Bingley was quick to see. Elizabeth's distracted air – for the picture of the gentlemen at port was so repulsive to her, with little to choose between Master Roper, the dreadful Mr Wickham, the preposterous Colonel Kitchiner, and only poor Mr Gardiner a true gentleman in all the company – gave Miss Bingley all the opportunity she needed, for she now remarked, in a sweet voice, that she was sorry not to have heard the end of Mrs Bennet's tale of a Frenchwoman.

"A Frenchwoman?" said Lady Catherine, looking up. "Which Frenchwoman would that be, pray?"

"Not *the* Frenchwoman," said Miss Bingley, with a knowing look at Georgiana – who this time looked away, uncomfortable. "An acquaintance of Mrs Bennet, Lady Catherine."

"Ah yes," cried Mrs Bennet, who was always happy to have any affliction, of the nerves or the body, and any remedy, however unproven, to be discussed at length: "I recall perfectly. To ensure a boy – I am told a douche with vinegar is just the thing!"

"This is advice we will not forget," said Miss Bingley – who threw a mocking glance at Elizabeth as she spoke.

"I am driven to my bedchamber," said Lady de Bourgh, rising.

"This advice must be useless to those to have not secured a husband," said Elizabeth with spirit, "and equally so for those who have lost one. Mama, I advise in turn that you take yourself to bed and rest, tonight – I will stay with Jane."

"I think we are not needed here," said Miss Bingley, rising also.

The party thus retired at an earlier hour than usual – but not before a report of driving snow in the park at Pemberley had made a necessity for Elizabeth of arranging for the Gardiner party to stay overnight. It was unpleasant, exceedingly so, to think of Darcy returning the following day to find Mr Wickham under his roof; but it could not be helped.

# Twenty-seven

Jane was in considerable pain; her labour progressed but slowly; and after Elizabeth had sat with her an hour – with Dr Mason ever in attendance, and Charles Bingley, whiter in the face than Elizabeth had ever seen him, pacing the ante-room and coming in from time to time – she resolved to go to her room and try to sleep a while. Leaving instructions that she should be woken if there were any developments in her sister's confinement, she went down the corridor and turned to go into her room – then, on an impulse, opened the door of Darcy's room and went inside.

Since their marriage, Darcy had inhabited his room very sparsely indeed; and it was empty and cold, with the curtains round the four-poster bed tied back to the posts as if in recognition that their proprietor would no longer find any use for them. The curtains at the window were also drawn back so that a new moon shone in, with a star at the tip, over the snowy park and trees. Pemberley lay in a deeper hollow now, with the snow all around it; and Elizabeth feared suddenly that its master would not return; that he was hurt, or had fallen, his horse prey to the monstrous accumulation of snow in the lanes between here and Matlock. Elizabeth sighed, and went to stand by the bureau, where pens and quills and paper were laid out, for the use of Darcy's correspondence, each sheet engraved with the picture of Pemberley House and coat of arms of the Darcys, entwined with those of the great line from whom Lady Catherine and Darcy's mother, the late Lady Anne, were descended; and she sighed again as she looked out on the moonlit park and wooded hills that were her new demesne.

For some reason she could not define, she recalled Lady Catherine's strictures, on her visit to Longbourn, that Pemberley – or the shades of Pemberley – should never be polluted by such as Elizabeth and her mother's family. And she smiled and thought of the times she and Darcy had laughed together at the insolence of his aunt. She had to confess, also, that she *had* brought some pollution to the place – for Mrs Bennet was so infinitely at her worst, here, and furthermore, without so much as asking her daughter, had invited the dreadful Colonel Kitchiner to the house. Perhaps, thought Elizabeth, there are truly those such as Lady de Bourgh who know best in these matters: perhaps Darcy's marriage to his cousin Miss de Bourgh would have brought him greater happiness – for there would have been an absence of pollution then – and Miss de Bourgh's fortune, to keep the air even cleaner; and he would not have gone off in an ill humour, as Elizabeth knew full well he had, in consequence of the vulgarity of his mother-in-law.

But Elizabeth's spirits were low and now she told herself she should go to her room and rest – for she must be ready for Jane – and, more importantly, she must keep Mrs Bennet from attending her sister. She was fatigued; that was it: the ill manners of Miss Bingley and the new attachment formed by Charles's sister with Georgiana had proved dispiriting; and both strength and courage were needed tonight. Tomorrow was Christmas: the birth of the Saviour would be marked by the birth of a child to her dear Jane – as modest and lovely as any mother could be; and this gave her strength, at a time when the shades of Pemberley seemed indeed to have all turned against her.

Elizabeth went to the door and walked out quietly into the corridor. To her surprise, she saw Georgiana, in her nightgown, standing by the door of her room. Her face bore an irresolute expression – Elizabeth glimpsed her before she was seen in return – and, as the girl heard a footfall coming towards her, she started and stepped back.

"Georgiana?" said Elizabeth gently. "What is the matter?"

"I am come to say I have been most ungracious in the last

days," replied Georgiana; and, as she was then overcome by tears, she permitted Elizabeth to put an arm around her and lead her into her own bedchamber.

"My dear Georgiana," said Elizabeth – and here a maid appeared, sleepy-eyed, to brush her hair and was told with equal gentleness to go off to bed. "My dear sister, when we are young so many new notions come into our minds – we take against people and for people – and, truly, Georgiana, you have full licence from me to feel as you do."

"But why, Lizzy, why are you so good to me?" cried the girl, kneeling by Elizabeth's chair at the side of the fire, which burnt still brightly. "I do not mean to mock Mrs Bennet, I give my word I respect your mother and am led to all this without knowing where I go!"

"Lady Catherine warned that Pemberley would be polluted by my mother," said Elizabeth gravely – and at this both she and Georgiana burst out laughing. "Now, my child, go off to bed – and think of it no more."

Georgiana showed by her shy embraces and smiles that her sister-in-law had restored her to calmness. As she went to the door, Elizabeth said: "I would like to ask you something, Georgiana. Do not answer me if you cannot."

Georgiana replied that she would answer anything she was asked. "Though there cannot be any secrets from you here, dear Lizzy – you have brought such a clear, fine air to Pemberley."

"I ask if it was possible that Darcy was in the village at about three after noon today," said Elizabeth. "For I swear I saw him there when I walked in to enquire of the party for the children of the men who work the land here."

"I do not think so," said Georgiana – very quickly, as Elizabeth noted. "He is gone to Matlock; the parson has died and he must find another incumbent for the living."

"Then I am mistaken," Elizabeth said; and, embracing Georgiana once more, she closed the door and prepared herself for sleep.

But it was long in coming. She waited, half of her alert, for the summons to Jane's childbed; and, for the rest, a puzzle lurked that she could not solve – for the reason that she could not know its nature. There was the dreadful episode of Mrs Bennet's recommending a douche – Elizabeth's eyes opened wide at this as she recalled it and she blushed there, alone, in the darkness – there was the talk of the Frenchwoman – and then, surely, the look Miss Bingley had given, at another Frenchwoman spoken of, but without a name. There could be no answer to this, and no rest if she were to dwell on it; so at last, when Elizabeth had banished from her mind the recurring picture of Darcy's return and his discovery of both Wickham and Colonel Kitchiner at liberty under his roof, she slept.

# Twenty-eight

For all the instructions she had given to be woken with news of Jane, Elizabeth's first understanding of her sister's ordeal came from Mrs Bennet.

"I told Mrs Reynolds to see you were not disturbed," said she in triumph, "for you do seem fatigued, my dear Lizzy, and I am in agreement with Miss Bingley – your looks are going fast – good heavens, when a young woman gives birth so many times, as I fear poor Jane will, she may be counted on to be worn out at thirty – but you have not even started yet!"

"How is Jane?" said Elizabeth, who found herself pinioned by the weight of her mother at the foot of the bed, and unable to move.

"She has been delivered of a boy!" said Mrs Bennet, producing and then wiping a tear from her eye. "And I do not wonder, Lizzy, that you show no sign of doing the same! Is it an accident that Mr Darcy finds himself called away on business? Do you wish for Master Roper to inherit Pemberley, all because you lack the desire to please? What amusement do you make for him here, that will keep him at home and interested in you?"

Elizabeth could not reply that the presence of her mother was likely to have brought about the instant attention to the filling of a parsonage some miles away that had become apparent to Mr Darcy; so she said nothing.

"You should be a great deal more agreeable," said Mrs Bennet. "Often you do not smile at all – or you tease him in a most impudent manner. I would not be surprised if Mr Darcy stayed away and did not come back in time for the Pemberley ball! For you will call for reels and the like and pay no respect to the traditions of the occasion – as Lady de Bourgh said only last night, you have not enquired once as to how *she* managed the ball. She does not know what the neighbours will think if it is all over the place, as she knows it will be if left in your hands."

"Mama, what nonsense! How can a ball be all over the place, when it will take place in the ballroom at Pemberley?" said Elizabeth, laughing. "But I must go to Jane now – I am so happy for her."

"It was feared that it would be a breech birth," said Mrs Bennet with great solemnity. "But the infant righted itself at the last moment. Dr Mason said poor Jane would have been in the greatest danger otherwise."

"And Charles? He is overjoyed, I have no doubt."

"Oh, I think a man will always be glad to have a son, Lizzy. I know your poor father was disappointed five times, and my accouchements were made none the easier for me at the sight of his long face, I can assure you!"

Elizabeth here thought of Mr Bennet, and of the love she and her father had had between them; and she thought with compassion of her mother, also: for had not the marriage of Mr Bennet and Mrs Bennet deteriorated so sadly, and had not Mrs Bennet been the constant target of his wit, she would most certainly have suffered from less vacuous a nature than was now the case.

"Mrs Reynolds tells me there is news from Matlock," said Mrs Bennet, as Elizabeth dressed quickly for her visit to her sister. "The roads are clearer than was thought, and Mr Darcy comes at any time to spend Christmas with us."

"Why did you not tell me before?" cried Elizabeth, who was ashamed to find the old joy at the prospect of seeing Darcy outweighed her happiness at the birth of Jane's child. "I was anxious for him," she added, as Mrs Bennet looked up at her with pursed lips.

"Then you must show it, dear Lizzy – fly to him now – look, I see him come down through the park. I do hope his horse will not stumble in the snow."

Elizabeth ran to the window. Mr Darcy did indeed

approach, but he was still some distance away, and relief at his safety was soon supplanted by an urgent desire to kiss Jane and compliment her on the birth, before he was at the west entrance to Pemberley.

"Lizzy, before you go" – and here Mrs Bennet restrained her daughter with a hand flung on to Elizabeth's arm and fastening there – "do tell me that you approve my new friend." Mrs Bennet batted her eyelashes exceedingly as she said this; and Elizabeth, confused with so short a night's sleep, succeeded by joyous news of Jane, and Darcy's return, professed herself unable to capture her mother's meaning.

"Colonel Kitchiner, my dear Lizzy! You know he asks me to be his wife!"

"This is not the time," said Elizabeth distractedly. "Surely, Mama, we can speak of it later!"

"You care so little for the future of Kitty and Mary!" cried Mrs Bennet. "Kitty may not find so delightful a husband as George Wickham – if she finds one at all; and I have no hopes whatever for Mary! Do you know she is all the time in the library with young Master Roper reading and talking of books – and I can see no prospect of her meeting anyone who will give her a dance at the ball!"

"Do not let us think of the ball now, Mama," said Elizabeth.

"Colonel Kitchiner wishes to provide for the girls. I would have thought that, as their sister and as mistress of Pemberley, you would ask of Mr Darcy one small kindness – which I know would encourage Colonel Kitchiner to proceed, as I know is his intention, with his proposal of marriage."

Elizabeth now left the room, her mother hastening after her. "Lizzy, there is no need to run! The baby Bingley will not go away! No – all I ask, my dear daughter, is that you consider the chapel at Pemberley – "

"The chapel?" said Elizabeth, stopping in her tracks. "Whatever do you mean, Mama?"

"Lady de Bourgh informed me of the existence of a chapel here, Elizabeth. I did not divulge to her the reason for my enquiry, for I know approval must be obtained first from

Mr Darcy – for our nuptials – so that Colonel Kitchiner and I may become man and wife here at Pemberley!"

Elizabeth would have laughed, but for the look on her mother's face. Of course there was no question of this taking place here. Her mirth, suppressed as it was, turned to anger. She knew not how she gained Jane's room, for she ran, with Mrs Bennet calling plaintively after her, and it was only after several minutes that she could rejoice in the quiet glory of her sister, and embrace her, and peer in at the sleeping child.

Mrs Bennet gained the hall, as Elizabeth and Jane smiled and spoke in whispers, and handed each other and Charles Bingley the infant to hold. Little Emily Bingley ran in with a nurse, to meet her brother, and time passed so happily that Mr Darcy had dismounted and walked in the door to Pemberley House before Elizabeth thought to run down the stairs to greet him.

Mrs Bennet was there before her, however. "My dear Mr Darcy," she called out to her son-in-law, "there are glad tidings! A son is born at Pemberley!"

# Twenty-nine

The following hour was taken up with talk of the weather. Shortly after Mr Darcy's return, the snow resumed falling, with deeper drifts, and wilder flurries, than before; and the roads impassable, so that the Christmas service at the village church could not be reached by the Pemberley party. The carriage, prepared for the Gardiners and Wickhams, had to go back to the stables. The phaeton would have been of no use at all.

Elizabeth could find no time to be alone with her husband, on account of the diverse plans and cancellation of plans which must take place, in view of the threat of the Gardiner party's being stuck here, perhaps indefinitely. She could see he was in an exceedingly ill humour; but this was hardly surprising; for Mr Wickham followed Mr Darcy around with a false and obsequious manner, reminiscing when it was least wanted on aspects of their shared past, and talking of Mr Darcy's late father with a familiarity that was odious to him. Lydia, also, who hoped for an allowance greater than the one already generously granted by her brother-in-law to her family, took pains to praise everything at Pemberley – so that Elizabeth did not know where to look, in shame.

"Oh, Darcy, I declare I have never seen such furniture as you have at Pemberley! Why, it is truly magnificent! I believe that, if Wickham and I had a dining-table and chairs half as fine as these, there would be an offer from a wealthy merchant to have us as his advisers. You know, to guide him in manners and furnishings and the like!"

"Hush, Lydia," cried Mr Wickham, who failed to see the extent of his host's displeasure, and cornered him neatly at the far end of the long gallery. "Darcy, I hear you seek an incumbent for the parsonage at Matlock. Will you not consider me for the place? Truly, I have led an exemplary life for many years now."

"You should see Wickham go down on his knees and pray each night," cried Lydia in an insincere voice.

Mr Darcy made no reply to this. Going from the long gallery to a drawing-room – and Elizabeth was sadly aware that she followed him as the rest did, as a subject might in hope of an audience with a rarely glimpsed king – Mr Darcy saw his aunt at her embroidery, and stopped to ask if the snowstorm had affected her repose on the preceding evening. Lady Catherine replied that the storm had left her undisturbed; but that other events had caused her to suffer a sleepless night.

"We will speak later," said Darcy gravely; and walked on, stopping suddenly as a crowd of small children – comprising the Wickhams and Emily Bingley – swept down the long gallery from the far end, whooping and crying as if in imitation of native warfare.

"Darcy, we should speak now," said Lady de Bourgh, rising.

Elizabeth was mortified in the extreme to see her husband and his aunt go into an ante-room and close the door. She now bitterly reflected that she had no sense any longer of her responsibilities. Where was the trust and affection between master and mistress of Pemberley that was the only hope of the continuance of a family party there without anger and resentment? "Darcy chooses to call off the entertainment for the children that was so near to my heart, on which I worked and planned for so long. Now he consults Lady de Bourgh, as to what to do with my poor aunt and uncle Gardiner, who had no wish to find themselves living on his charity, for they are proud, good people. But then, he has to put up with Wickham as his brother now. I do not wonder that he turns from me and talks to his aunt. And he returns to find a baby just born here. Oh, it is not to be thought of! Jane should never have come, so near her time! It was Mama's selfish want of her – and now we are all exposed to Mama's foolish ways."

So thought Elizabeth, her mind in turmoil; and seeing Darcy come out of the ante-room with a face like thunder, and Lady de Bourgh very straight and tall behind him she did for a moment think of running from the house and away altogether.

This impulse, however, could not have been carried through even if she had wished it, for the figure of Colonel Kitchiner now appeared at the head of the stairs and advanced to join the assembled company, each member of which was now struck dumb at the realisation that Mr Darcy had not the slightest idea who this gentleman might be.

"Ah, Colonel," cried Mrs Bennet – but then stood as silent as the others as Darcy turned his eye on the uninvited guest.

Certainly Colonel Kitchiner did not cut a dash. His apparel, stained from the excesses of the dinner table and the port of the night before, was unkempt in the extreme; and, walking as he did with a sideways limp, on account of his wooden leg, he gave an air of being escaped from a house for the insane. It was noted that his eye glittered and his jowls moved at great velocity, in his desire to make himself known to his host. Master Thomas Roper followed him at a short distance.

"Mr Darcy," said Colonel Kitchiner, coming forward and attempting a bow which all but swept him off his feet, "it is my very great pleasure to make your acquaintance!"

Here Darcy did turn to Elizabeth. She saw not a gleam of amusement in his eye; she saw him as an offshoot of his aunt: icy, arrogant, proud. And her spirit rose in her, to say in as cool a tone as she could find that she wished to present "Colonel Kitchiner, a cousin, visiting from Manchester; and snowbound here like the rest."

Darcy did not hold out his hand. Lady de Bourgh, with an awful expression, returned to her chair; and Master Roper commenced a lecture on the campaigns in the Peninsular Wars in which the colonel had participated; along with a full description of artillery and musketry deployed.

Colonel Kitchiner was not to be deflected by Master Roper's intervention. He came closer to Mr Darcy – who now stood up by the window, looking out impatiently at

131

the falling snow which kept all the party under his roof, and spoke right into his face as if addressing a person devoid of hearing.

"We are connected, Mr Darcy, I believe. The Mortimer Moores, of Devon, had Salway House; and a Miss Darcy was married from there to Mr Mortimer, my great-uncle, on my mother's side. Yes, indeed."

"So we are related twice over!" cried Mrs Bennet, coming up to Mr Darcy with as great impunity as Colonel Kitchiner had done. "We are cousins all along! Lizzy, do you hear that?"

Mr Darcy showing no sign whatever of having heard this, the party then dispersed. The weather made any expedition outside imprudent; rooms were opened up that were not customarily in use, and fires lit – for Lady de Bourgh, as became clear, had requested of her nephew that new apartments be made available to her, Miss de Bourgh and Miss Bingley alone. On discovering this arrangement, Elizabeth's cheeks burned; but what could she do? She could only wish herself swallowed up and a million miles under the ground, rather than endure the meal to which they would all go in at four o'clock.

# Thirty

The house now contained all the different members of a family which did not yet in itself exist. Thus thought Elizabeth, for the shrieks of the children were audible still; and the disapproval of Darcy's aunt seemed to look down on her from the portraits on the walls and miniatures set out on the tables. Pemberley had become a shrine to the lasting qualities of a name and a fortune and an estate, and it did not care for diversions, only for continuance. And this, Elizabeth thought at last and bitterly, she could not provide. The benign features of the late Mr Darcy, as he appeared to Elizabeth's gaze in the higher gallery, which was quiet now with the dispersal of the ill-assorted group to their separate quarters, asked that she give Pemberley the means to live on, in comfort, without disruption, in a straight line from himself and his son. The more distant portraits, of Jacobean Darcys, and of boys and girls in lace collars and with spaniels at their side, from the ancient line to which Lady Catherine and the late Lady Anne belonged, asked as well this one simple thing: if Darcy, in his life span, was no more than steward of Pemberley, its acres, outlying farms, villages and churches, then was it superfluous to ask of his wife that she provide an heir? Was Mrs Bennet, even, right in thinking the attitude of Elizabeth the reason for her barrenness? Was it not true that, in her joy and relish at her time in this paradise alone with Darcy, she had given little thought to her duties, as mother of the future of Pemberley?

These thoughts were sombre indeed; and Elizabeth found herself oppressed by the seemingly endless reminders of her husband's progenitors. It was as if there were no other family in England, or none of half so great an interest, at least, as the Darcys; and that this was also likely to be true made the sense of near suffocation all the more pronounced. But that there was nothing in the world that did not find itself measured against the Darcys, and was then found wanting: this was the cause of Elizabeth's sense of oppression, and her sudden yearning for escape, for a place where she would not be known and not be judged. For was she not expected to be chatelaine of this great place, and overseer of the good of the village; and mother, too, to poor Georgiana – when she was not yet three and twenty? It was too much; and, seeing the snow had stopped falling and sun shone beyond the walls of Pemberley, Elizabeth threw on a cape and, choosing a door that led into the garden from a remote part of the house, went out.

The park was dazzling in the whiteness – and as Elizabeth followed a path made there by estate workers and not entirely covered over by the recent falls, she heard the children cry out with delight, as they were permitted to run in the snow, build men there, and throw balls which slithered the length of the icy stream and broke up against the bank.

Elizabeth walked quickly, and was not seen by them. Soon she found herself winding up to the left, among trees; and there, in a clearing which gave a view both of the village and of Pemberley House, stood Mr Gresham, occupied in axing a tree.

Elizabeth and Mr Gresham greeted each other cordially. As the cries of the children outside the house could be heard; and their bright figures could be seen, the size of marionettes, below, she could not help but see Mr Gresham smile with pleasure at their antics; and she could not prevent herself, either, from comparing his toleration and amusement with the stern anger of her husband at sight or sound of the Wickham and Bingley children as they ran and played. Was Mr Darcy immured in a generation, such as his aunt Lady de Bourgh's, where children must be treated with the utmost severity, must be regarded as inheritors of a title or estate, or destined for church or army – or, in the case of female children, the hearth and the cradle – was this the cause of Darcy's rigid attitude?

If so, she had married a man who belonged, truly, to the old world, and she was as far from him as if he and she dwelt on different planets. The thought made her cold. Was it a whim, stemming from his basic indifference to children, that had caused the sudden cessation of the children's party? Did he have other ideas for amusement, which conflicted with the date Elizabeth had set for the entertainment? It was too horrible to think of. Elizabeth recalled the words of Miss Bingley and Lady Catherine, of the day before. Did they know? Why should they not know? Darcy detested children; and all along they had known it, if she had not.

To break the silence, companionable enough, between them, Elizabeth asked Mr Gresham why he removed the tree – did it do any wrong there? – and then laughed at her words, the young estate carpenter joining her with a spontaneity clearly expressed in his pleasant, open features.

"It is a birch that is half eaten away," said Mr Gresham, "and the other trees will be infected by the rot. So I take away its agony! See . . ." And he held out a fungus, huge and of an orange-yellow colour, that would have caused anyone with a less strong stomach than Elizabeth to recoil.

"I confess I have taken a wrong turning," said Elizabeth, when the fungus had been hurled from the clearing by Gresham and could be heard falling into bracken and snow. "I thought to walk up to the tower, where the imprisoned queen went to watch the hunt – I must have gone quite another way!"

"Yes – this is in actuality the highest point of the village," said Gresham, gesturing to a cluster of thatched cottages just visible through the trees. "They are not habitable any longer; they are about to be demolished; and the remaining residents relocated further down, by the blacksmith's cottage, where you go, Mrs Darcy, to make your arrangements for this year's festivities at Pemberley."

"Which no longer take place," said Elizabeth quietly. "So how many people have needed to remove from this place?"

"Only two – old Mrs Benton, a widow who was put in charge of the lad when the Frenchwoman died – " Here

135

Mr Gresham stopped short and coloured. "It was impassable here in winter, as you can see, with snow, and in spring, with mud from the stream bursting its banks when it comes down – "

"Who," said Elizabeth, "who, Mr Gresham, was the Frenchwoman? For I have heard talk of her at the house," she added quickly, for fear Mr Gresham would see her own colour come and go. "I am interested to hear more of her. She was the mother of a child – whose child?"

"Mrs Darcy, I cannot answer," said Gresham, "I am not cognisant of the facts. I give you my word on it."

"Would the child be a boy of about six years old?" said Elizabeth. "When did the Frenchwoman die, Mr Gresham?"

"It must be three years ago or thereabouts," said Mr Gresham, who now looked very miserable indeed.

# Thirty-one

Elizabeth was back at the house in time to go to her room and change, in preparation for dinner. She lay instead a long time on her bed, before deciding she must go and see how her infant nephew and his mother fared. To find Jane, as she did, in radiant good spirits, with Charles hovering at her side – and then departing for the orangery, to bring blossom to a room already fragrant with the lilies Mr Darcy had sent up from the greenhouses; to see the happiness between the pair at the birth of their son, was healing to Elizabeth, for she put the welfare of her sister above her own, and had often declared that, if Jane were ever to suffer in life, the sufferings of her younger sister would be greater still, at the injustice of it.

She had so lately been in great pain that it was a wonder to Elizabeth to see Jane in the full bloom of her beauty and health; and when Charles had left to go and play a game with little Emily – it was to be a form of hide-and-seek, for which Pemberley was perfect – Elizabeth sat in a sofa at the end of the bed and poured out all that was now in her heart. It was the contrary of the life she had now, this calm tranquillity and domestic delight, such as was enjoyed by her sister and Charles Bingley. It was wrong of her, she knew, when Jane must be fatigued from giving birth – but she had such need of her. "Oh, dear Jane, forgive me – but I am bewildered by all that I have learnt – and you should rest, you should give all you have to the child and not to your wretched sister, as I am selfish enough to ask."

"Hush, Lizzy," said Jane, "there is room enough for me to love you both – and look, he sleeps! Tell me what has befallen you." And, in a tone that was more grave, "I trust our father was not right, when he expressed incredulity at your intention of marrying Mr Darcy! I do not think so – for I have seen you happy together – but it is not easy. No, I see that. He has his pride still, and all favour of his office, and fawning courtiers in anyone he meets, to keep him proud. You *have* softened him, Lizzy; but when Lady Catherine comes – and, for all you have kept from me, I imagine dreadful scenes with her and Mama – he is put on his pinnacle again and he finds he has lost the way to come down from it."

Elizabeth here told the tale – of Georgiana's shame at siding with Miss Bingley – "and I believe there was something else, which she did not have the courage to tell me. I believe Miss Bingley put her up to letting out the secret of the Frenchwoman, with the purpose of upsetting me," said Elizabeth with a sigh. "Tell me, Jane – did *you* ever hear of a Frenchwoman – did Charles ever speak of such a woman, living here in the village?"

"No, never," said Jane. "You know, Lizzy, it is not like Mr Darcy to hide something of this kind; I cannot believe a word of it."

"But the child," cried Elizabeth. "I saw him distinctly – he had a child with him, in the village. And now Mr Gresham tells me this Frenchwoman had a child, and died three years back. Oh, Jane – she was his love! He lost her, he has the child who can never be to him what he most craves. It is for this that Darcy detests children – his heart is broken, that is why!"

"Elizabeth!" said Jane, who was most concerned now at the distracted air of her sister, and the certainty of her pronouncements. "Can you recollect that once you believed all you were told of Mr Darcy by a son of his late father's steward, Mr Wickham?"

"Yes – "

"Mr Gresham has not the character of George Wickham, I am convinced; but he is also the son of the steward: who can tell what *his* motives may be, in telling you secrets from the past of Pemberley? You judged once too quickly, Lizzy – must you again?"

"You are right," said Elizabeth, after a pause. "You are

wise as ever, my sweet Jane. Yet – my thoughts are in turmoil – why cannot I ask him outright? What is it in his nature that would frown so on this, that I would feel banished from his affections at once? Oh, if only I could talk to our father of this, Jane, and hear what he has to say – "

"You know he would make a jest of it," said Jane, "and you would not find it easy to laugh this time, for your future is bound up with Darcy, and not with him. Reserve your judgement, if you can – and the truth will emerge – for it has a way of doing so."

Charles here came in and said that dinner was in the banqueting-room tonight – as Darcy had ordered it so – and that he must dine with the company and would be up presently to see his wife and infant son. "There has been no repeat of the snow, at least" – for Charles was sensible to the difficulties that were Elizabeth's lot, as hostess of this party – "and the carriage will take the Gardiners and the Wickhams to Rowsley in the morning. As for Colonel Kitchiner, I escort him to the main road, where he may get the stagecoach to Manchester."

"And what of Mama?" enquired Jane, as she lifted the sleeping baby into her arms. "Will she permit this?"

"Mrs Bennet is engaged in preparations for the New Year's Ball," said Charles, smiling; "and she has asked Mr Darcy that Colonel Kitchiner should come to Pemberley for that; permission which has kindly been given."

"So all is well," said Jane, smiling up at her husband.

# Thirty-two

Elizabeth did not know how she would get through the dinner. The banqueting-room she and Darcy had never sat in when alone, not even on the rare occasions when neighbours were invited to Pemberley. The candelabra on the long, polished table, the immensity of the room, with high leaded windows, the chandeliers which threw shadows on the trees and swards, ruched dresses and silk breeches of the ancestors portrayed on the walls, combined to give her a sense of nausea, of dizziness: if it were not for Mrs Bennet's speaking of her affliction over twenty years, she would have said that she truly suffered from her nerves. There was so much to ponder, to fear. One minute, it seemed to Elizabeth, her future lay in ruins, the next that she dreamt the whole thing and would be happy with Darcy again tonight – for was he not back safely from his journey to Matlock in the snow? And his ill humour was gone; he laughed with his sister and Miss Bingley; and was even civil to the colonel.

For all this, Elizabeth could not forget the words of Mr Gresham; her imagination was haunted by the French-woman; her thoughts ran so loud in her head, she thought she spoke them: "Three years since she died! He came to Hertfordshire, when Charles Bingley rented Netherfield, soon after his heart was broken! Little wonder he had no desire to meet the belles of the country; hardly surprising that he cared so little for me at first, that he did not go to the trouble of asking for an introduction! Yes, he saw my fine eyes; later, he came to like my spirit, for I would not fawn on him, as all the others did who hoped to wed him, to reign as queen in his court. But as a man would prefer the company of another man – who would not make eyes at him, presume on his affections when he could feel nothing. His heart taken up with the tragedy of the mother of his child!"

Caroline Bingley, on seeing Elizabeth as far as she could be, in her thoughts, from the assembled company – and therefore vulnerable – looked down the length of the table and remarked, "It seems to be the time dear Lizzy is accustomed to go to bed at night – for she has left us for the Land of Nod, I swear it!"

At this, Miss Bingley laid her hand over Mr Darcy's and laughed heartily; but Elizabeth could see that Darcy frowned and pulled his hand away: Miss Bingley presumed too much.

"We would all go to bed at sundown when we were very young, would we not, Georgiana?" said Miss Bingley, who seemed now to wish to present herself as a considerably younger woman than she in fact was. "When we played Hunt the Thimble here, Fitzwilliam, and you joined in – do you not recall how sleepy the poor child became – and I was so overcome with weariness too that Nurse had perforce to carry us off to bed?"

Mr Darcy professed that he had no memory of this episode whatever.

"How can that be?" cried Miss Bingley, who was disconcerted at this. "Tell me, Lizzy" – and here she raised her voice again, so the other diners had no choice but to fall silent. "Have you observed that Mr Darcy is grown very forgetful since your marriage?"

Georgiana snickered at this, and Elizabeth found no difficulty in giving her reply.

"No, I have detected no absence of mind. But I have noted one fact, in general, and I am surprised that it has evaded your attention."

"What fact?"

"That there are those who, on attaining maturity, put childish things behind them," said Elizabeth gravely. "And there are those who never attain maturity and dwell for ever in their childhood for want of anything else to occupy their minds."

A silence ensued; and Elizabeth saw that Darcy, who was thoughtful at first on hearing this, was once again exceedingly good-humoured.

"Now there you have it, Caroline," he said. But Elizabeth, in her display of the independence of spirit for which she had ever been known, felt, as all her own memories of recent days returned to her, the old shadows descend on her again.

"Lizzy!" cried Mrs Bennet down the table. "You have been in such a reverie you have forgotten to answer dear sister Gardiner, who has been speaking to you ten minutes at least!"

Elizabeth started; and apologised to her aunt.

"No, my dear niece, I said only that we are grateful indeed for all the comforts Mr Darcy has provided for us! Did you know that Mrs Reynolds was instructed to bring us all fresh linen, and – in the case of Colonel Kitchiner, I believe – new coat and pantaloons too. Mr Darcy has given us a visit to Pemberley which we shall not forget, dear Lizzy – and he has said to Mr Gardiner that, as soon as the snow melts, he must return and fish the stream at Pemberley."

Elizabeth said she was delighted at the attentions shown to her family by Mr Darcy. As she said the words, though, she lapsed once more into her private world; she heard Master Roper, as he quizzed Colonel Kitchiner on the Peninsular Wars; and Lady de Bourgh, as she made a comment on the *grosse pièce* of the meal, a sucking pig on a great platter, with an orange stuck in its mouth. But she cared little, for it was not she who had given directions for this banquet but Mr Darcy – her own directions for a quiet Christmas evening had not touched on such grandeur.

"I am surprised that dear Mrs Darcy permits cheese to be served in the evening," said Miss Bingley in a high voice.

Master Roper now described in detail the battle of Borodino; and, as Elizabeth awoke and looked down the table, she saw Miss Bingley listening and talking with great animation – surprising to Elizabeth, for she had not supposed Miss Bingley to take an interest in military matters. There was a reason, though, as she soon discovered, for Miss Bingley was teasing Mr Darcy on his activities in the campaigns; and he seemed not in the slightest displeased by this – which, Elizabeth thought, was also unexpected.

"We chased them back to Paris," cried Colonel Kitchiner, who had arranged his knives and forks to represent the rout of Napoleon at the hands of the British. "The Froggies were running for their lives, I give my word on it."

"But Mr Darcy was back and forth and running in two different directions," said Miss Bingley slyly, "were not you, Darcy?"

"He was a spy for the English," cried Georgiana. "I was too young to understand at the time – my dear brother would be gone so long from Pemberley, and then he would return – and he had saved the lives of so many unfortunates, caught in the path of war!"

"And so that is how you found the Frenchwoman," thought Elizabeth, "and brought her back here to enjoy her more fully."

"What nonsense you talk," said Mr Darcy, smiling. "I made a few visits to Deauville and Le Touquet – but I went purely for my own amusement, I can assure you. My companion Mr Charles Bingley will vouchsafe that!"

"Sir, your reputation as a man of extraordinary courage preceded you everywhere in France," cried Colonel Kitchiner.

A weariness overcame Elizabeth, and she stood, to signal that the ladies should accompany her from the banqueting-hall. Mr Darcy smiled at her as she did so. A week or so before, she would have delighted in seeing his approval at her capture of the exact time for the separation of the sexes after dinner. Now she cared little if each and every member of the party stayed imprisoned in the room until the Devil came to take them. She was numb to feeling; she could not return Darcy's smile; she knew only that the detestation he had for children came from his own past – and that he was prepared to cancel the estate workers' children's party on a whim, because he wanted no more young voices in the house: they recalled to him, no doubt, what could have been. She had been chosen to come and live at Pemberley, as a man would choose a friend, a companion. He had never wanted a child with Elizabeth Bennet, and never would.

Elizabeth left Mrs Bennet in hot pursuit of Lady Catherine – who made every effort to gain her new boudoir without being perceived. She went to say good-night to Jane. Her sister slept – all was quiet, and the nurse watched over the crib. Elizabeth entered her own room and closed the door.

She sat long at the dressing-table, and, much later, turned away the maid who came to prepare her for bed.

The house, after sending up the sounds of people retiring for the night – doors closed, shutters were drawn together, footsteps sounded on the floors below – lay deep in stillness, punctured only once by the high voice of a small child, woken suddenly from a dream. Still she sat on, unable to bear her solitary reflection any longer, and turned on her dressing-table stool to face the door. For she heard Darcy's step now. It was unmistakable: firm, measured, but without assertion, the step of one who has trodden every inch of the house since he first learned to walk, and belonged there as unassailably as the pictures on the walls and the druggets of fine carpet which betrayed his coming.

Elizabeth saw the handle of the door turn, and she went to meet him. She could not admit him – her feelings ran too high for that – and she could not deny him admittance either; so she found, though she hardly knew what she did, that she took the key from the door and, as she went out, locked the door behind her.

Darcy, whose mood was genial in the extreme, looked for a moment puzzled; then, going down on his knees, he looked up at her and spoke part in earnest, part in jest.

"My loveliest Elizabeth, what are you thinking of tonight? Are we to sleep in an attic, to savour the novelty of it? Shall we abandon Pemberley and fly secretly abroad, leaving our guests to rule the roost?"

Abroad, thought Elizabeth bitterly; and she was unable to resist asking Mr Darcy if by "abroad" he meant France. "The French are no doubt most dear to you," she said; and

144

was surprised, herself, to find her eyes fill with tears. "Your Frenchwoman has very probably a sister there, to whom you can pay your addresses."

"What?" cried Mr Darcy, who had risen to his full height and no longer smiled.

"You cannot deny the existence of such a woman in your life," said Elizabeth, "nor of a child. I must know more of it."

Darcy's face darkened and he stepped forward, so that the couple, if anyone had spied them there from a distance, would have given the impression that an amicable conversation was in progress. "Elizabeth, there has never been another woman in my life. Not a Frenchwoman" – he tried to smile once more, but this he failed to accomplish, for it was clear he was wounded by her allegations – "nor a Dutchwoman, nor any other kind of woman, I give you my word! What is all this farrago of nonsense, I pray you tell me at once?"

Elizabeth did not wish to implicate the young librarian, who, as it seemed to her, had supplied this information, so she said nothing. Her heart beat uncomfortably; she did not dare look up at Darcy; but she did not entirely believe him either, for she detected a note of falsity in his voice that she had never heard before.

"Well?" said Mr Darcy, more calmly. "Do we go in to your bedchamber, or do we go to separate quarters? The decision is yours, my dear Elizabeth."

There was an impetuosity in Elizabeth which could not be checked; the mention of separate quarters set off a chain of reactions over which she found she had no control. She must speak – and speak she did, though Darcy's face became every minute colder and harder, and he stepped back from her in surprise and disdain.

"How dare Lady de Bourgh take it upon herself to demand a boudoir exclusively for herself and Miss Bingley?" cried Elizabeth. "And poor Georgiana, too, who has fallen into their clutches? Am I not the one to tell Mrs Reynolds where we shall go after dinner? Am I to be disregarded entirely?"

"You forget, Madam," said Darcy, with an ominous speed

of return, "that my aunt is driven to extraordinary measures this year at Pemberley."

"And what might they be?" cried Elizabeth, colouring up.

"Lady Catherine is not accustomed to share meals or drawing-rooms with such as Mrs Bennet," came the reply. "Nor should my sister be forced to sit with Mr Wickham. My aunt is aware, of course, that my love for you overcame the scruples I felt on the occasion of my first proposal of marriage to you, at Hunsford parsonage. She wishes to remain within the family, and respects that love. But she is not enamoured of you, sweet Elizabeth, as I am" – and here Mr Darcy came close and *was* smiling – "so it cannot be anticipated that she will tolerate your mother to quite the same extent that I do!"

All this was spoken partly in a playful spirit. Elizabeth, who had turned pale, now stood with her arms outstretched behind her, against the door.

"And now, at last, do we go to bed?" said Mr Darcy.

"No! I am patronised enough! My mother shall not be insulted by you and your detestable aunt any longer!"

"My dear Elizabeth, you put me in mind of the theatricals we were used to stage here when my sister was a child," said Mr Darcy with a twinkle. "Sweetest, loveliest Eliza, will you not let me in?"

Elizabeth, by way of reply, unlocked the door to the bedchamber, walked in and closed the door again, with no little vigour. As she did so, she saw Darcy's face and saw on it an expression of hurt pride that made her for an instant regret the spontaneity of her action. But it was too late; she could not forgive him; and she turned the key in the lock from inside. She went to her bed, and for a long time lay silent, until Darcy's footsteps were heard to go away. Then she wept, from sheer sadness – that the proof of Darcy's lack of real respect and affection for her was now, from the ease with which he delivered insults to her mother, only too plain to see.

# Thirty-three

The following day saw the departure of the Gardiner party for Rowsley; and of Colonel Kitchiner, escorted by Charles Bingley to the main road to wait for the Manchester stage-coach. Elizabeth made her farewells with every outward show of calm; and repeated many times that she looked forward as much as the rest to the ball at New Year's Eve; and Mr Darcy, who was as genial as a host who bids farewell to uninvited guests can be expected to be, did not linger in the hall when they were gone – as would otherwise have been his wont – to talk and jest with his wife. He went directly to the steward's house, across the park, to see to the management of his estates; and left instructions with Mrs Reynolds that he departed himself that night for London, to see to his interests there at Holland Park.

"London!" cried Mrs Bennet, on receiving this news, as the rest did, on going up to the long gallery after the carriage carrying the Gardiners and Wickhams had gone out of sight. "Good gracious, Elizabeth! Does he not take you with him?"

"I trust Mr Darcy can see to his properties in London without taking his wife every time with him," replied Elizabeth in a faint voice – for it was as much as she could do to remain calm after the shock of this news. "He has often said he is much needed in London; and I saw that this morning brought mail; no doubt he did not find the time to tell us all at leisure of his plans."

"Mail there was indeed," said Lady de Bourgh.

"I believe there is a fine new opera opened in London," said Miss Bingley – who was not slow to understand that

147

something was amiss between Mr and Mrs Darcy – and to show she was glad of it. "And urgent business at Boulestin's after, I dare say."

"Oh, how I wish I could go to London," cried Georgiana, showing her seventeen years in the sudden yearning in her voice. "It will be dull here, without Darcy, and the ball will be nothing without him."

"There will be no ball," said Lady Catherine. "My nephew found time to inform me of his decision to leave for London and not to hold the Pemberley ball this year – even if he did not find time to tell dear cousin Elizabeth."

"Excuse me, Madam," cried Mrs Bennet, who felt the need to protect her daughter – as Elizabeth saw, much to her discomfiture. "I am sure there is a good reason for Mr Darcy's failing to tell dear Lizzy. She is always slow at her toilet in the morning – that is it – and with the press of people leaving for Rowsley and Yorkshire and the rest, he was unable to find a minute alone with her."

"Mama, please . . ." said Elizabeth.

Her thoughts were in a spin, and Mrs Bennet's efforts made it all the worse. For she recalled, with such violent freshness of memory that it could have been but a day before, how she had hated Darcy when she had first seen him! – how Charles Bingley had described his friend as the most dreadful of beings, when bored on a Sunday evening with nothing to do at Pemberley! She saw now that every evening was become a Sunday evening to him, and that he saw his marriage as a farce. His pride meant that one occasion of her flinching from him – and who would not, when he had so blatantly expressed sympathy with his aunt on the matter of her boudoir, not to mention the secrets lately implied by Mr Gresham? – had him turning away from her and going all the way to London to be as far from her as possible!

To add insult to injury, he had told his aunt, and not her! Oh, it was too much! *He* had not changed, when they exchanged vows: *his* pride was as evident as when they had first met, at Netherfield! But then why should it be thought that, when two people went to live happily ever after, they *would* do so, unless they understood themselves and each other better? And Mr Darcy – why, he had not even tried!

Elizabeth was mortified to feel tears prick her eyes; and to receive an amused glance from Miss Bingley.

"It is to be considered fortunate that there will be no ball this year at Pemberley," said Lady Catherine in sepulchral tones. "For we would have found ourselves in the invidious position of welcoming under this august roof an unprincipled scoundrel – two of them, indeed!"

And what has he not cancelled? thought Elizabeth bitterly. Any event that would give pleasure, whether to the children of the men who work here so loyally for him; or to neighbours and friends, for whom an evening at Pemberley is the high point of the year, that is the sad truth of it. Why does he do this? Because he feels no happiness and pleasure in himself: he still grieves over the woman he loved: he cannot bear for people to laugh and show their merriment, any more than he can withstand the laughter and romping of little children!

"I do not speak only of Mr Wickham – now, alas, joined to the Darcys through marriage," said Lady de Bourgh. "I speak of the supposed Colonel Kitchiner."

"How dare you, Madam?" said Mrs Bennet, whose awe for Lady de Bourgh was exceeded by her desire to think highly of her unprepossessing suitor. "The Colonel may not be a whole man – "

"He is certainly not a whole colonel," said Lady Catherine stiffly.

"What can you mean, Lady Catherine?" said Master Roper, who had been looking through a folio brought from the library by Mary Bennet. "I believe you have evidence to support my suspicions."

"I paid a call yesterday on the Dowager Countess of Mornington, at Mornington Park, not three miles from here," said Lady de Bourgh. "Colonel Fitzwilliam, a close relative of ours, is a guest there for the season. I asked him a simple question. Colonel Fitzwilliam was able to answer me without hesitation. In short, my dear Elizabeth, Colonel Kitchiner is not and never has been attached to the – Regiment."

"What?" cried Mrs Bennet.

"He was certainly not at the battle of Borodino," said Master Roper, "for I posed him several questions on that campaign – nor did he lose his limb in warfare, for I was able to ascertain that the method of fixing a wooden leg such as his has been quite superseded. It is probable that Colonel – I beg your Ladyship's pardon – *Mr* Kitchiner was injured in a fall some years ago, suffered the loss of his leg, and never fought in the Peninsular Wars at all!"

"Eliza!" cried Kitty Bennet, who had giggled at this with as much enjoyment as Miss Bingley and Miss Darcy, who were convulsed. But she now saw her mother swoon. "Lizzy, go to Mama! Oh, Mary, fetch the smelling salts! Oh!"

"I have never extended my charity to those unable to control their emotions in public," said Lady de Bourgh, as poor Mrs Bennet was taken by Elizabeth and her sister to a sofa, the window opened, and a glass of cold water called for. "I should have thought Mrs Bennet would be grateful to hear the true origins of Mr Kitchiner – who, Colonel Fitzwilliam informs me, is a tradesman in a seaside town. Are these the kind of people to be given free admittance to Pemberley?"

# Part Four

# Thirty-four

A few days after this, the party at Pemberley dispersed. Without Mr Darcy, the guests showed themselves ill at ease; and for all the fare, and the celebration of Christmas, there was widespread relief when it was over.

Miss Darcy went to stay with Miss Bingley in London, where they thought to see Darcy and involve him in their amusements. Mrs Bennet informed her cousin in Manchester, Mr Kitchiner's sister, that she would come and visit her, for a short duration, for, as she said to Elizabeth, "whether he be a colonel or not, he has offered to settle eight thousand pounds on the girls."

Lady de Bourgh and the silent and sickly Miss de Bourgh, accompanied by Master Roper, departed for Rosings, "where tradition has it that a discreet gathering takes place to mark the New Year; I expect to receive a visit from Mrs Fitzmaurice, whose family has been as long as ours in the country."

Jane and Charles Bingley, with their children, were the last to leave. They took with them Kitty and Mary Bennet – for neither showed the slightest inclination to stay at Pemberley with no ball to make ready for; and Elizabeth was left alone in the house, but for Mrs Reynolds and the servants. She frequently passed by the portrait of Mr Darcy in the picture gallery – the very portrait she had first seen, when brought for the first time to Pemberley by her aunt and uncle Gardiner – and she recalled perfectly the expressions of admiration the picture had elicited; for he was handsome indeed, hanging on the wall. She did not stop, however, or indulge her feelings by looking up at him; nor did she go to the table where the miniatures of Darcy and Wickham stood, in a salon kept ready for her, but never used. Mr Darcy was everywhere about: it

153

was hard enough to reclaim her own sense of herself, before contemplating a grim future.

The library was the only part of the house where Elizabeth could regain a memory of what she had once been – however fleeting this memory inevitably proved to be. She had been happy, at home as a child; a library brought tender thoughts of her father; and the fact that this new addition to the famous Pemberley collection of books and folios was dedicated to him brought her at least a fond memory of Mr Darcy, also – for he had respected the dignity of Mr Bennet and wished to show the world he did so. These thoughts often proved painful in the extreme – but they were preferable to the imaginings by which she was visited, if she walked into the village, or stayed in her bedchamber. Here, at least, was the calm of books; the impartiality of tomes written by authors long dead, who lived on still in this house, where everything that had been of value to her had died.

Mr Gresham was often in the library. He supervised the last stages of carpentry, and was as happy in his habitat as Master Roper had been pompous and overweening. He was an avid reader, but did not flaunt his scholarship. Elizabeth felt him, also, to be drawn to her; for he coloured exceedingly when she came in, past the pillars of the new annexe; and frequently she felt his eyes on her, as she selected a book to read, or searched for her father's favourite works.

There was no harm in spending time with Gresham – so Elizabeth reasoned with herself. Was it not a pity that Pemberley, where he had spent his youth just as much as Mr Darcy – should go, not to him – who knew every inch of house and land so well – but to Master Roper? Was it not permissible, when she had been left to occupy herself as best she might by a disaffected spouse, at the saddest time of the year, for her to enjoy his company, when soon he would go south to resume his studies – and, after that, might never come to Pemberley again? Was she to be walled up here, like a wife in the Gothic tales she had so derided when she was a girl? Most telling, was she not still young now, and in need of a charming companion of her own age?

Whatever reply she gave to herself, even this ceased to be an option. Mr Gresham received instructions from London that he should go there immediately; he was to work for architects employed on the scheme for a crescent in Holland Park that was to be built by Mr Darcy on his land; and there was no time to waste, as he must be of assistance before he returned to university. Darcy had been nothing if not fair. Elizabeth admitted this with a heavy heart. He would take what he wanted from those who were his dependants, but he would not stand in the way of their freedom. Hers was a case not dissimilar to Gresham's: Darcy had wanted from her an unconditional love she had not found herself able to give; now he left her free to decide how she would pass her life, without imposing himself further on her. She must have sighed, for Gresham came over from the window where he stood examining an illuminated manuscript, and smiled at her.

"It would be good for you, Mrs Darcy, if you would take a change of air," said Gresham gently. "Why do you not go south, when I go? I shall be happy to escort you."

"No – I am asked to London," said Elizabeth, to whom it had become second nature to make this pretence, in order to satisfy the curiosity of retainers and neighbours, many of whom were surprised to see Mrs Darcy quite alone at Pemberley at this time of year. "But I hope to resume my charitable work in the village" – here her eyes could not meet Gresham's, nor his hers – "and I intend to set up music lessons, as before, for the musically gifted children of the workers on the estate."

"You should go south and see the spring – it takes long to come, here," said Mr Gresham.

After he had departed, the days did indeed hang heavy at Pemberley. Elizabeth determined to visit Jane, for although there was a young baby to care for, and all the domestic duties concomitant with this, she felt the want of a friend and confidante desperately. She would go only for a short visit: to see her sister's happiness, and hear her wise counsel, would restore her spirits; for soon, she knew, she must decide on a course of action that would take her away from Pemberley and all the memories of eager anticipation the place held for her.

The Bingleys were well settled at Barlow, and, if Elizabeth

found Jane a little pale, she ascribed it to the inhospitable north-ern climate and to the rigours of recent childbirth. The house was warm and agreeable; little Emily's toys were everywhere about – but, as Elizabeth was to discover as she found her way again round the rooms, there was no sign of the child herself.

"You will not find her here," said Jane, when both sisters were seated by a fire and drinking tea. "Emily has left for Whitby today, to take the sea air. The nurse goes with her. She has been most unwell – but she improves and the fever is gone. Now all that is needed is the return of the roses in her cheeks – poor mite!"

Elizabeth expressed concern and asked what had ailed Emily; and, as she did so, she felt keenly her exclusion from the world of childhood illnesses and recoveries: from life itself, as it did more and more appear to her, since the sound of children clapping and singing had been stopped at Pemberley, with the cancelling of the party. Only the shrieks of the young Wickhams had been there, Elizabeth recollected grimly, and *that* had been enough to stifle any maternal longings.

"Why, Emily was a victim of the influenza," said Jane with some surprise. "Did not Darcy tell you – that this was the reason for cancelling the party at Pemberley?"

"Why, no," said Elizabeth, and she saw her sister note that she coloured up violently. "I was told nothing of this."

"There was an outbreak in the village," said Jane, "and Darcy was concerned that the children would make themselves worse if they were exposed to cold and snow on the way to the party – for they wanted so much to come. He was right, I believe, although they had so much looked forward to the occasion. Little Emily succumbed to the influenza only when we had returned here – I would not have travelled with her in such a condition!"

"But why did not Darcy tell me?" cried Elizabeth. "He tells me nothing at all – except to insult me on the subject of poor Mama!" And here, to her own discomfiture, Elizabeth broke down in tears and confided the story of Lady Catherine's part being taken by her nephew, to Elizabeth's everlasting mortification.

"But Lizzy," said Jane, when she had come to the back of her sister's chair and leaned over her and kissed her, "Darcy did not wish to alarm you, when the influenza was at its height in the village, and it seemed some of the children might lose their lives!"

Especially his own child, thought Elizabeth.

"He knew what love and attention you had given to the concert – he could not bear to see you burdened with anxiety, when you had us all at Pemberley. And now, for all the trouble over Mama and Lady Catherine – Darcy has plans in London that will make ample repairs!"

"What can they be?" said Elizabeth, and found she could no longer look at her sister candidly.

"Darcy confided in Charles," said Jane, with the simplicity of manner her sister had all her life trusted and loved. "Before he left Pemberley, he swore that he would never forgive himself for his insolent remarks about Mama. He designs a house for her, in London, in Holland Park, where she can give a ball this summer for Kitty!"

"A house?" said Elizabeth – but, for all the gratitude she was intended to feel, she knew only the sadness of her situation. True, she had misjudged Darcy over the cancellation of the entertainment for the children of the men on the estate. And she could almost smile at the thought of his efforts to improve the position of poor Mrs Bennet. But the past; the ghost of the Frenchwoman and the child that was no ghost at all – these she could never banish from her memory.

To Elizabeth's further mention of the Frenchwoman, Jane could only respond with patience and a hint of reproof: "Lizzy, you dwell too much on the past! Leave Pemberley; come and stay with us for as long as you wish. Please, dearest Lizzy!"

"I shall leave Pemberley," said Elizabeth, as the infant Bingley was carried in and Jane resumed her motherly duties. "But I shall not come here to burden you with my troubles, Jane. I need time to think – to breathe – away from Pemberley. But it must not be here!"

# Thirty-five

Elizabeth returned to Pemberley in low spirits. The sight of the village children, who waved to her as she went past, recalled to her the kindness shown by Darcy in sparing her the cruel facts of the influenza. She knew she had misjudged him. Yet go she must – and as soon as a destination could reasonably be decided upon.

Elizabeth's prayers were answered – or so it appeared – when, on returning to Pemberley, she found a letter on her table in the sitting-room. It was from Charlotte, the friend of her youth who had been Charlotte Lucas and was now Mrs Collins, and she smiled at the kindness of the wish expressed within its pages:

My dear, very dear Eliza.

How long it is since we have seen each other! You will know, perhaps, from your Mama that I expect a child in the spring. I long for your news – how grand it must be at Pemberley! Mr Collins tells me of it every day – though I believe he was there only once for a few hours, when Lady Catherine stayed with Mr Darcy. Most of all, how is Mr Darcy? Is your marriage all you dreamed of, Lizzy? I am quite positive it must be. Oh, if only you could come here and visit us! But Mr Collins tells me there are so many engagements in Derbyshire at this time, to which Mr Darcy and yourself are committed – that you would never have time to come to Longbourn! In the spring, perhaps? For we enjoy a very mild climate at present, and daffodils are coming up ahead of time.

Charlotte ended with such expressions of affection that Elizabeth stayed a long time, reading and re-reading the letter. Longbourn – where she had passed her childhood – Longbourn, which might be unbearably changed since Mr Collins had settled there. But it was still Longbourn, filled with memories of Mr Bennet and happy days. And Mrs Bennet was not at Meryton Lodge; she was in Manchester.

Elizabeth wrote to her friend and announced her arrival at Longbourn House.

# Thirty-six

Every stage in Elizabeth's journey gave her a fresh sense of freedom, and of hope. Pemberley lay behind her, very dark on a day that threatened more snow, and was already wet, so the chaise was several times stuck in the mud. But Elizabeth could reflect that the Hertfordshire mud, towards which she travelled, was of an altogether different hue from that of Derbyshire: that she would feel herself renewed by sights once so familiar and now not seen for so long; and that she would put this chapter behind her, however hard it might be – though it was too late, it was true, to laugh it off, as she might have done had she and Mr Darcy fallen out prior to the marriage instead of later.

Still, she left no outstanding debt behind her. There was no one who would cry for her, at Pemberley, even if it meant she must admit Georgiana Darcy had once seemed to her as dear as a sister. No – Georgiana was Mr Darcy's sister, not hers. She had gone to London with Miss Bingley, to meet the fashionable people Darcy had always proclaimed he despised. Aunt and uncle Gardiner would come down from Rowsley none the worse for their visit to Pemberley – though Mr Gardiner would not now get his day's fishing. Had he not said on the occasion of their first visit there that great men such as Mr Darcy were too prone to change their minds and act on whim – that he would not take the first invitation to try his line seriously, unless it were offered a second time? He had not been mistaken. The second invitation *had* come, but bad weather had stood in the way, and now there would not be another. Mr Darcy was not likely to continue his acquaintance with such as the Gardiners.

Mr Darcy had done no more than act on a whim, so Elizabeth thought as the chaise carried her further from Pemberley. He had repented his arrogance towards Mrs Bennet; and he had used, doubtless, the excuse of business interests in London to conceal his intention of designing a house for her mother, to entertain in; but it had not been so very much more than a whim, after all. He could not know what she had deduced from Mr Gresham of his past; he was exasperated by Mrs Bennet, and no doubt by Master Roper also, and certainly by the huddle of people marooned two nights under his roof when they had not been invited for more than refreshment and a tour of the park. But was this enough to justify a departure so cruel and sudden, without informing her – leaving her at the mercy of his aunt's superiority and Miss Bingley's triumph? More and more it seemed to her that, if this was not a whim, she could not define it better. For could a single argument end a marriage – or announce an estrangement, at least, which was the effect of Mr Darcy's departure? He was bored with her and he went to London to seek happiness elsewhere: that was all.

The journey was long. But, when the lanes of Hertfordshire showed themselves, Elizabeth cried out with delight – the twist in the road, the palings of the park, all received her at Longbourn as if she had not been long gone. The chaise stopped outside the front door, after traversing the gravel sweep; and Elizabeth could even resign herself to the fact of Mr Collins's coming out on to the doorstep, instead of her father. Before she had left the chaise, he had his speech under way. Only Charlotte coming out and laughing at him to allow poor Elizabeth to alight and recover brought his list of obsequious greetings to a halt.

Elizabeth saw instantly that her cousin's manners were not altered by inheriting the house and estate where she herself had spent her childhood with her sisters. He detained her on the step some minutes, to ask details of the welfare of Lady de Bourgh and Miss de Bourgh; and then of her family. He led her – just as she thought the hall and Charlotte's sweet presence as confidante and friend lay before her – to look at the new currant bushes he had put in behind the house, in a garden walled off from the rest – an idea he had obtained from Lady Catherine on her return from a visit to Scotland. At last, he allowed Elizabeth into the house – and repeated several times that Longbourn must appear small and humble indeed, to one accustomed to Pemberley. "You are more than welcome," said Mr Collins. "You will find some curtains and chair covers that will surprise you – designs taken from Rosings, when my dear Charlotte and I were at the parsonage. Lady de Bourgh was kind enough to permit Charlotte to order a cretonne exactly identical to hers."

Elizabeth admired everything she was shown; and was at last taken to her room – which, she saw with a pang, had been Mr Bennet's – and Charlotte came to offer tea and help her unpack her bag.

Elizabeth now heard of Charlotte's happiness, and her expectations of motherhood. "I shall be so well appointed here, at Longbourn! The upper floor shall be for myself and the baby – I have put pictures and prints up there for the sweet creature to look on pretty things as soon as he is born – although I hope" – and here Charlotte blushed – "I do hope for a daughter, Elizabeth!"

Elizabeth said she knew Charlotte would make an excellent mother. If she noted to herself that Mrs Collins had placed herself in future upstairs with the child, rather than in the nuptial chamber with Mr Collins, she did not remark on it.

"But I feel ashamed," cried Charlotte. "I boast of my happiness. Now I want to hear of yours! Your Mama has been round here, speaking of the jewels and carriages your marriage to Mr Darcy has brought you! And joy also, I hope, dear Lizzy, for you do deserve it, you know! We have had a letter from Mrs Bennet" – here Charlotte's voice dropped, and she looked attentively at the carpet by the side of her chair. "Is she entirely well? She appears . . . overwrought. But I dare say it was the excitement of visiting Pemberley."

"Yes, I dare say," said Elizabeth.

"She spoke to Mrs Long – I know this is indiscreet, but

you will find that Meryton has not changed – of becoming engaged to a major in the army. Is this true?"

"A colonel," Elizabeth corrected her friend, before recalling that Mr Kitchiner was nothing of the kind. "But I do not think anything will come of it, Charlotte."

"Tell me of life with Mr Darcy," Charlotte cried. "I cannot wait! You are the envy of all the country, you know, Lizzy!"

Elizabeth told the story; and Charlotte's face grew ever more grave as she heard it.

"A Frenchwoman? Living in the village with his child? I do not believe it! It cannot be true!"

Elizabeth spoke of Mr Gresham's credentials and sincerity in such a way as to leave no doubt in the mind of her friend.

"But what will you do, Eliza? What will become of you?"

Elizabeth replied that she would go to teach children: "I am good with children, I earnestly believe," she said simply, "even if I am barren – "

"Oh, do not say that, Lizzy!"

"I intend to devote my life to the education of children who have not been favoured by circumstances."

"Mrs Darcy a teacher! Mrs Darcy a governess! Impossible!" cried Charlotte.

"It is not impossible at all, my dear Charlotte. I have written to a Mrs Wood in London, a good friend of my aunt Gardiner; and I shall go there from here. I have the name of a good woman who cares for orphans in Hackney; and my work may well take me for years at a stretch out of England."

"Oh, this is dreadful," said Charlotte, who now began to weep.

Elizabeth said gently that she did not find it dreadful at all. "What would be unimaginable would be to spend another minute of my life with a man so detestable, so filled with a monstrous pride and insolence, as Mr Darcy."

"Oh, I never thought to hear this!" cried Charlotte.

Elizabeth embraced her friend and suggested they go into Meryton after she had changed her clothes and bathed – "for we did enjoy walking there together, Charlotte, did we not, when we were young?"

"Yes, yes – we shall go today, for tomorrow the doctor comes to me at Longbourn. I would so like you with me, for my own comfort, Lizzy!"

"Does not Mr Collins attend you?" said Elizabeth.

"Oh, he will, Lizzy, if I ask him! But he tells Dr Carr at such length of the difficult birth that was had by Lady de Bourgh with her daughter Anne – and which her ladyship had intimated to him, but without giving any particular, of course, that I am barely looked at at all!"

"Then we shall go to Meryton today," said Elizabeth. And she rose, to continue with unpacking her bag and making ready for the trip.

"My mother will be overjoyed to see you!" cried Charlotte. "She wishes to hear everything of life at Pemberley!" Here Charlotte paused and looked downcast.

"And how is Sir William?" enquired Elizabeth, for she wished to help Charlotte out of her awkwardness. "Your father is in as good health as Lady Lucas, I trust?"

"Certainly," said Charlotte. "Indeed, he is recently returned from the court of St James, and he reported that he spoke with Mr Darcy there. We thought you must be in London," she added, before falling silent once more.

# Thirty-seven

Meryton on a winter's afternoon was just as Elizabeth recalled it. She was struck by the differences between a southern town and a small town in Derbyshire, such as Matlock. And, even as she went along, she found herself back in Derbyshire again, living her new life with Darcy and going to visit her sister Jane.

But it was not to be: Meryton it was. After a look at the milliner's – for Charlotte was set on a hat – the friends stopped at Lady Lucas's, to take a dish of tea.

"We have all missed you here, dear Mrs Darcy," said Charlotte's mother, as she offered them seats by a hospitable fire. "But we know your position at Pemberley is such that you cannot easily be spared."

Elizabeth coloured and said nothing; Charlotte stared intently into the fire.

"I received a letter from your dear Mama only yesterday," continued Lady Lucas. "She did not know you intended to visit Longbourn, I suppose?"

Elizabeth said it was indeed true that Mrs Bennet had left Pemberley before she had decided to come south.

"And you did not think to tell her!" said Lady Lucas. "Well, married daughters must keep themselves to themselves – I am fortunate that Charlotte still confides in me as if there had never been a marriage with Mr Collins!"

I am not surprised, thought Elizabeth. To confide in Mr Collins would be quite unthinkable.

"At least she will be most pleasantly surprised, when she comes to Meryton Lodge, to find you so near," said Lady Lucas.

"Does she come soon?" said Elizabeth, who tried to hide her alarm.

"Indeed she must be on her way," cried Lady Lucas, "for she brings news of such a happy development. I am sure you know it, dear Mrs Darcy, but Mrs Bennet has sworn me to secrecy."

At this moment Sir William Lucas came in. He was followed by Mrs Long, who had seen Elizabeth in the street with Charlotte and could contain herself no further.

Sir William Lucas greeted Elizabeth by bowing low, and remarking that he had lately been at court and seen Mr Darcy there.

Elizabeth could think of nothing to reply to this, so she said nothing. Sir William talked of the court of St James's so frequently, she wondered if he would not haunt it after he was dead. This state, she was sorry to admit, she sincerely wished him in as he continued with his well-worn pleasantries; and, in order to calm the feelings that were stirred up in her by mention of Mr Darcy, she pleaded a headache and said she would like to go back to the house and lie down.

"My dear Lizzy," said Charlotte, full of concern, "you do look rather pale. We will get Papa's carriage to take us back – it is too far to walk."

Elizabeth was about to demur when Mrs Long asked – with a certain slyness – how Mrs Bennet had enjoyed her seasonal visit to Pemberley. "I believe she expected a visit from a cousin of yours, Mrs Darcy – a cousin of both of yours, I should say. She was most intrigued to meet him – I wonder if he came!"

"Oh, he did," cried Lady Lucas. "I have it here in Mrs Bennet's letter. A Colonel Kitchiner! I always did imagine that a woman so good-looking and agreeable as Mrs Bennet would find a husband when she had not been widowed long."

Here Lady Lucas stopped, on seeing Elizabeth, and recalled her affection for her late father; and it became clear to her also that Mrs Darcy had actually been present when Mrs Bennet's new suitor had appeared at Pemberley.

"So, how is this Colonel Kitchiner?" said Lady Lucas. "If I may be so bold as to ask you, Mrs Darcy?"

Elizabeth was provoked by the ill-breeding shown in this manner of question, and rose abruptly.

"Mrs Darcy, do not leave," said Mrs Long. "I have the temerity to ask if your mother Mrs Bennet handed to you a small token made for you as a Christmas offering."

Elizabeth said she regretted she had no recollection at all of being handed anything that came from Mrs Long.

"Oh, it was merely a trifle," said Mrs Long, who eyed Elizabeth sharply and decided against continuing with this line of conversation. "Something small – I made it according to a pattern that came down from my mother-in-law" – she could nevertheless not prevent herself from running on: "Charlotte, it will do perfectly for you!"

"I cannot think what it can be," said Charlotte smiling.

"For the baby," said Lady Lucas, "was it not, Mrs Long? I recollect you making a perfect little smock and giving it to Mrs Bennet."

Here Lady Lucas and Mrs Long did not look into each other's eyes and a silence fell. Shortly after, Mrs Long took her leave.

"Now we are all family," said Sir William, "for, Mrs Darcy, I must count you a cousin now that Charlotte has married into Longbourn – we await your reactions to the momentous news in Mrs Bennet's letter of yesterday."

"I would not dream of telling Mrs Long," said Lady Lucas with a virtuous air.

Elizabeth was finally compelled to confess she had no idea what Mrs Bennet's news could be – though she dreaded what she thought it *must* be; and that was the approaching marriage of her mother and Mr Kitchiner. She would be asked for her blessing – and she would not be able, she knew, to grant her mother's wish. Taken up with these distressing thoughts, she did not properly hear Lady Lucas's next words.

"She will be twice the dowager of Pemberley!" said Sir William, in agreement with his wife. "Mrs Bennet may well take precedence over Lady de Bourgh at St James's now, would you not concur, cousin Elizabeth?"

"What is that?" said Elizabeth.

"Why – that Miss Mary Bennet will marry Master Roper! They had no sooner been separated, at the end of their visit to Pemberley – than Master Roper wrote to propose marriage to Mary! And she always in her spectacles too!" cried Lady Lucas. "Mrs Bennet is in seventh heaven. But she did not know you were gone from Pemberley; she must have written to you there – that must be the reason!"

"Mrs Bennet will be delighted that, whatever may happen," said Sir William in a solemn tone, "her line will continue at Pemberley!"

Elizabeth expressed herself astonished at the news; but said she wished her sister and Master Roper well.

"They are for ever in the library, Mrs Bennet tells me," said Lady Lucas.

"The Darcy family is known for a strong interest in the arts," said Sir William. "Why, only the other day, in London, I saw Mr Darcy come out of the opera house with a young lady – a singer or dancer, I would wager – and the lady who was the sister – at Netherfield?"

"Miss Bingley," said Elizabeth.

# Thirty-eight

The following day, Elizabeth was reading in the parlour when Mr Collins came in and addressed her in a manner which was unfamiliar to her.

"My dear cousin Elizabeth, it is with the very greatest delight that I welcome you to Longbourn. I wish you to be fully aware of this."

Elizabeth replied that she much appreciated the chance of being in her old home again; and of renewing acquaintance with Charlotte's relatives and other residents of Meryton.

"We set no limits on the duration of the visits of our guests. At Rosings, it goes without saying, Lady Catherine can hardly permit herself this lax approach: she has dignitaries of all kinds as visitors; and even the Prince, I believe, has stayed at Rosings."

"Indeed," said Elizabeth, who could not see where this conversation was leading.

"*She* has to delineate the dates and expectancy of the duration of her guests' abode with her. *We* may extend to a cousin such as yourself a more generous portion of time than it would be in her ladyship's power to appoint."

"I can certainly give you a day for my departure," said Elizabeth, "if this would be of assistance to you, Sir."

"It could be helpful," said Mr Collins. "Dear Charlotte will be confined – as you know – and Sir William and Lady Lucas have done me the honour of accepting an invitation to stop over here during this time. I have much to attend to here. You have seen the new woods I plant at Longbourn, I trust?"

Elizabeth replied that she had barely had the opportunity of inspecting Mr Collins's improvements.

"The park here is very small," said Mr Collins, "but it will have its scope enhanced greatly by the woods – all of miniature trees – which I plant in the form of battles. Over there" – and Mr Collins strode to the window and pointed to the empty park – "there will be Waterloo! A perfect formation of the troops, with the defeat of Napoleon symbolised by a leaning tree supported by timbers. And a line of trees against the horizon – the retreat from Moscow! What do you think of it, cousin Elizabeth?"

Elizabeth said she thought the idea was very fine, though she found it hard to keep a straight face.

"My heirs will know how Mr Collins marked his age at Longbourn," said Mr Collins.

Elizabeth thought of the enjoyment her father would have had, at this ridiculous proposal; and then she thought how he would have hated the despoliation of his park; and she sighed.

"Cousin Elizabeth, I know your afflictions. You will understand that I have sympathy for your plight. Our Lord extended his pity to Mary Magdalene. I may do the same for you."

"What?" said Elizabeth.

"It is painful to discuss these matters further," said Mr Collins. "I hope you will not be inconvenienced by moving from your room today. It must be prepared for Lady Lucas; and both Charlotte and I know you will prove most adaptable. We have made up Mrs Moffat's old room – it is behind the kitchen, as you know – and we are sure you will be most comfortable there for the remainder of your stay."

If Elizabeth had not understood Mr Collins at first, she now saw only too well what had transpired. She learnt much on the subject of marriage. For Charlotte, her good friend Charlotte, had confided her secrets to Mr Collins, as Elizabeth did not think she could. And yet, why should she not? She was his wife. She had married, not for love, but to get herself a husband and a home: none the less, her first loyalty was to her husband and she had told him of Elizabeth's estrangement from Darcy, her lack of a secure future. Mrs Darcy was a poor relation now. Mrs Moffat had been housekeeper at the time of Mr Bennet. To be moved to her room could only be seen as a reflection of this.

"You may regret certain of your decisions," said Mr Collins, with an odious smile. "If you recall, cousin Elizabeth, I was punctilious in the extreme when it came to consideration of your family at Longbourn. I wished to keep your mother happy, and your sisters with a roof over their heads. I asked for your hand in marriage. You may repent at leisure the course of action decided on then."

"Mr Collins," said Elizabeth, rising from her chair and going to the door, "I shall pack my bags and leave Longbourn immediately."

Here Charlotte came in and asked if the doctor had come yet, for she fancied she had heard voices in the hall.

"Cousin Elizabeth informs us regretfully that she leaves us today," said Mr Collins.

"No!" cried Charlotte, whose sense of friendship and hospitality was shocked. Elizabeth could see she was sincere, and that nothing had been concocted between husband and wife to effect her removal from their house. "Lizzy, you shan't go yet! Why, you have only just come!"

The maid came in and announced that Dr Carr had arrived.

"Oh, I had better go upstairs now," cried Charlotte. "Lizzy, you look so pale, you should see Dr Carr when he has finished with me. Promise you will!"

"I should like a word with the medical man myself," said Mr Collins, "for I feel a fit of sneezing come on, when I plant my trees. He must supply me with a tincture, for I cannot read a book when sneezing – it blows away all the pages!" With this, Mr Collins left the room abruptly.

Elizabeth and Charlotte did not look each other in the eye. Charlotte was agitated, and came to throw her arms around her friend.

"I did not mean to do you harm, Lizzy! Mr Collins has spoken to you, has he not? I did not mean to tell him so much. Promise you will stay – as long as you wish!"

But Elizabeth, after promising that she would come and see

171

Charlotte in an hour's time, when she had been examined by the doctor and had had her rest, said only that she would go for a walk and return to say farewell to her friend. It was a fine day; she would set out in the direction of Netherfield.

# Thirty-nine

The walk across fields to the house Mr Bingley had rented when first he came to Hertfordshire recalled painfully to Elizabeth the time Jane had been ill at Netherfield; how Mrs Bennet had prayed her eldest daughter would catch a husband, as well as a head-cold, by riding out in the rain in the direction of the house where the eligible Mr Bingley had decided to reside; and how Mr Bingley's sisters had jeered at her muddy shoes and the hem of her skirt that had trailed in the puddles. It was painful – today was as wet on the ground as it had been then. But she needed to reflect; to return to the place where she had first met Mr Darcy; and to confront her future with some of the courage and candour she imagined her sister Jane would bring to a similar situation. She must learn not to be hurt by the remarks of such as Mr Collins. She must leave this world, with its fashion and conceits; she must find herself by caring for others.

So thinking, Elizabeth stopped by the gate that led into the park at Netherfield. She saw it was unlocked; and she walked through into long grass that had not been grazed by cattle or sheep in months, if not years. Was Netherfield Hall not let, then? were her words, and the music on the piano, and the games of cards they had all played of an evening, preserved here, not supplanted by successive tenants until they were no more than a shadow in the fabric of the house? It was a ghostly thought; and Elizabeth shivered as she walked up through the park to the parterre, and the garden – also overgrown and neglected. It was a fine day, cold and bright. She would not linger, but she would permit herself a glimpse of the ballroom, where she had first gone in hope of meeting

173

Mr Wickham – and the recollection sobered her further. She could recall – yes – the snub administered by Mr Darcy, that she was only tolerably good-looking, and certainly not worth being introduced to; she could smile at the picture of Jane dancing with Mr Bingley. But she had found Wickham agreeable in the extreme, had she not? And, leaning forward and staring in at the dark and empty room, the chandelier and unpolished parquet floor of the room where the future had first shown itself – for the two Bennet girls at least – she was bound to admit she could be as wrong as anyone, when it came to love.

Elizabeth walked quickly away from Netherfield. When she arrived at Longbourn, Dr Carr and Charlotte were in the hall – Charlotte bade him farewell until the following week. She cried out in alarm when she saw her friend. "Lizzy! You are shaking with the cold! And you are not well. Have you seen a ghost? I have never seen you like this."

Dr Carr was pressed to give relief to Elizabeth – who was indeed half fainting from the effects of her expedition to Netherfield Hall. He escorted her gently to her room as Mr Collins looked on, shaking his head and remarking repeatedly that he had pressed dear cousin Elizabeth to stay indefinitely at Longbourn and not to tire herself as she did.

# Forty

Despite all the pleas of Charlotte, Elizabeth announced she would leave Longbourn the next day – when a good night's rest and the ministering of her friend had taken away some of the strain of the preceding days. Mr Collins, who came to her room to offer apologies, was thanked, but firmly dismissed. Only his information that Mrs Bennet was known to have returned safely from Manchester and was now ensconced in Meryton Lodge caused her to postpone her departure for London, for a short while. For it would be inconceivable to go directly from Longbourn to London without visiting her mother. Besides, Mrs Gardiner's friend Mrs Wood had not replied to Elizabeth's letter yet, and she did not know if she had lodgings to go to, in London.

Charlotte wept when Elizabeth accepted the offer of the pony cart, to go down as far as Meryton; and begged her for the hundredth time to overlook her indiscretion with Mr Collins.

But indiscretion it was not, thought Elizabeth, as she waved farewell from the trap. Marriage is such; there are no secrets in a marriage – except in mine.

Mrs Bennet received Elizabeth coldly. "I do not know which room you will have, I am sure! Mary comes today, from Barlow – Kitty goes to Lydia and they all go to Bath, where she will find more amusement than there was at Pemberley, that is for certain. Mary shall have the room next to mine. You had best go in the study, Lizzy!"

Elizabeth said that she was happy to sleep anywhere. She would leave for London soon, and wished to be no trouble at all.

175

"You will see Mr Darcy in London, I hope," said Mrs Bennet.

"No, I go to aunt Philips, if she will have me," came the reply.

"Aunt Philips! You are the most foolish and wilful girl I have ever known! What would Mr Bennet have said of this scandalous behaviour? What will become of me, if you and Mr Darcy are estranged? Will he want to keep me on in Meryton Lodge? Have you considered this, Elizabeth?"

Elizabeth admitted she had not. Nor was she disposed to fluster her mother further with tales of a town house in Holland Park and a fashionable season; when Mrs Bennet was accustomed only to Bath. However, this was the time – and she knew she must not flinch from it – to ask Mrs Bennet of her matrimonial intentions. "Did your visit to Manchester go well, Mama? Do you still intend to wed Colonel . . . Mr Kitchiner?"

"Mr Kitchiner is the most arrogant, insolent and detestable man it is possible to meet," cried Mrs Bennet. "I would not dream of marrying him – and I told him so outright."

Elizabeth could not refrain from a sad smile at this parody of the state of her own feelings for Mr Darcy.

"His sister is as conceited and vain as he is," continued Mrs Bennet, "and they are venal too, the pair of them! I would have ended without a stick of furniture or the clothes on my back! They had a scheme that I sign over my four thousand pounds to them now – and receive an annuity, with the residue to go after my death to my unmarried daughters. They are scoundrels, Lizzy – and I will thank you to allow no mention of Mr Kitchiner or his sister in Meryton ever again."

Elizabeth said she would tell no one in Meryton; and that she would not be there, in any case, in the foreseeable future.

"Thank goodness there will only be Kitty now, to wear out my nerves," said Mrs Bennet, "and I have told Lydia she *must* see that Kitty gets suited in Bath – with whomsoever it may be! And for all the sorrow you have brought to our family, Elizabeth, I can at least rejoice that my visits to Pemberley will continue regularly."

"What do you mean, Mama?" said Elizabeth, who was startled to hear this.

"Why, with the marriage of dear Mary and Master Roper, to be sure! It is as much like two book-worms meeting in the binding of an old folio as anything I have ever come across! He will change his name, I suppose – I have not asked him this, but I think Roper-Darcy would be fine, do not you, Lizzy? For Mr Darcy goes to the Continent – so Mary wrote to me, from Barlow. He must have told Charles Bingley. And Mary and Thomas will live at Pemberley."

"Oh," said Elizabeth – and could say no more, for she wondered that Jane had told her none of this; and then the thought that she would never see Darcy again came in on her painfully.

"Mary is young – but it is a good age to start a family," said Mrs Bennet, "and I shall wait on Mrs Roper-Darcy for as long as she wishes me there."

Elizabeth went to the study, where a bed was put up by the maid with a good deal of grumbling, and she sat long there, contemplating the ruin of all she had most desired. Darcy going away! Pemberley with Mary as its mistress! She could console herself only on the correctness of her discoveries about Darcy. He goes to France, she thought miserably – and doubtless he takes the child with him.

Her reveries were interrupted by a tap at the door, followed by Mrs Bennet coming in greatly agitated.

"Lady Catherine de Bourgh is here, Lizzy! I expect she brings a letter of reconciliation from her nephew! You cannot receive her in here – you shall have the sitting-room – it looks out on the park – which is smaller even than the park at Longbourn, I am aware. But that must be laid at the door of Mr Darcy, for it was he who fixed up this accommodation!"

Elizabeth was sickened, both by the news of Lady de Bourgh coming to find her here; and by her mother's chatter. She went into the sitting-room, as there was nothing else to do about it, and found Lady Catherine standing with her back to the fireplace. Elizabeth greeted her formally and asked her to take a seat.

"I shall do nothing of the kind! I am here to inform you that you must go to Mr Darcy immediately!"

"And why should I do such a thing?" said Elizabeth.

"I see you are as impertinent as when I first came to see you in your father's house. Your departure for Hertfordshire without informing your husband of your destination was ill-considered in the extreme!"

"He did not inform *me*, before he went to London."

"My dear Mrs Darcy, that is quite different! My nephew was informed of the whereabouts of his wife by some upstart at St James's."

"Sir William Lucas," said Elizabeth, smiling.

"You must mend your marriage – or at least be seen trying to do so. It is understood that you will not bring an heir to Pemberley – "

"Understood by whom?" said Elizabeth.

Lady de Bourgh stopped, and stared hard. "Do you tell me you are with child?"

"What if I am?" replied Elizabeth.

Lady de Bourgh was for a while speechless; then she asked if Elizabeth would come with her, to meet Mr Darcy.

"I am sorry if there has been awkwardness at court. There is nothing I could wish less on Mr Darcy," said Elizabeth sweetly. "But I intend to pursue my own plans, as before."

"And what may they be?" cried Lady de Bourgh.

Elizabeth would not, however, divulge her intentions to Mr Darcy's aunt, and showed her to the door.

# Forty-one

Mrs Bennet's exasperation with Elizabeth was soon forgotten, when Miss Mary Bennet came from Barlow. As future mistress of Pemberley, she was greeted with open arms, and a splendid repast was laid out in the dining-parlour.

"You may join us, Lizzy, I suppose," said Mrs Bennet. "Oh, how I do wish Mr Bennet were here, to compliment you on your engagement, Mary."

"He would be sorry to miss seeing his prospective son-in-law, Thomas Roper," said Elizabeth gravely.

"And tell me, when will dear Thomas come to Hertfordshire?" cried Mrs Bennet, on whom this irony was lost.

Mary said he would come south soon. He would go to Rosings first, and she was invited there by him, in a few weeks' time.

"Lady de Bourgh was here only today," said Mrs Bennet.

Elizabeth half listened to the chatter which followed; but she became alert suddenly, when Mary alluded to the poor state of their sister Jane's health.

"It is a fever of some kind – that follows childbirth, Lizzy. Poor Jane was ill ever since her return to Barlow, but she did not wish you to learn of it."

"Lizzy certainly does not know of the dangers of giving birth," cried Mrs Bennet. "My poor Jane – she has puerperal fever. Oh, this is dreadful!"

Elizabeth thought it was dreadful, too, that Mary only now alluded to her sister's dangerous condition. But she had also to acknowledge her own feeling of unease. Was this illness of Jane's not a direct consequence of her anxiety about her sister? Was her constitution, robust enough when not weakened by childbirth, now endangered by the secrets concerning Darcy and his departure for the Continent – secrets she felt she must keep from Elizabeth for fear of causing her even greater distress?

"I shall go to her," said Elizabeth, rising.

"But my dear Lizzy, it is quite dark!"

"I go at daybreak. Jane may be very ill," said Elizabeth, who was distraught with fear for Jane. "I shall make my arrangements and then go to the study and wait until it is light."

"If it were not for my nerves," cried Mrs Bennet, "I would come with you! But I cannot bear another journey when I am so lately down from Manchester!"

Elizabeth said she knew Jane would understand; and she left the room.

# Forty-two

The journey north at this time of year was even more hazardous and cold than the journey south; and Elizabeth's thoughts were correspondingly dark and troubled. What if poor Jane were to die? How could life be borne, without her? How could Charles go on, with no sweet presence at his side? And now I know, thought Elizabeth bitterly, how Darcy felt, when his lover died, and he was bereft. I must learn to forgive; and to pray for Jane without thinking of him.

Elizabeth was admitted to the Bingleys' house by the housekeeper, who wept as she led the way to Jane's room.

"She is so much weaker, today, Ma'am. The doctor comes again, but it is all to no avail."

Elizabeth went softly into her sister's bedchamber, and knelt by the side of the bed. Jane was weak and ravaged, indeed; but a smile spread over her face when she saw Elizabeth; then was chased away again, as if the phantoms of fever had precedence and could not be banished even by the arrival of the sister she loved most.

"She took a little broth earlier," said the housekeeper, "but she raves – do not hear what she says." And Elizabeth saw the poor woman was alarmed at her mistress's state. As Jane began to speak, she understood further the alarm just expressed. For surely Jane spoke from madness – or fever – her words came from nowhere, and yet she spoke with such conviction that it could only be the truth.

"The child – oh, if only you knew, Lizzy!"

"But I am here, Jane," said Elizabeth in a low voice.

"The woman was taken from the battlefield – oh, she was

wounded, I have no doubt – they brought her here. He loved her; I know that, too."

"Of what do you speak?" cried Elizabeth; and the agitation in her voice caused Jane's eyes to open and to look at her, for a moment, with the old candour.

"You *are* here. I did not dream it! Go to the door, Lizzy, and open it and go through. Stand at the top of the stairs. You can hear well, there."

"But what shall I hear? I will not leave you, Jane."

"You will hear of the Frenchwoman – who was the mistress of Charles Bingley – who bore him a child. Whom Mr Darcy so kindly protected, after the Frenchwoman's death. You know, Lizzy, when Darcy tried to prevent Charles from marrying me – he did it for this reason! He did not think Charles properly recovered from grief at the death of – "
Here, Jane's head fell back on the pillow, and she raved again, strange words and conjunctions with the sense and nonsense of nightmare.

Elizabeth's colour came and went; she laid a hand on her sister's brow, and cooled it with lavender water; she went at last to the door, and out to the top of the stairs. Her mind was in turmoil. Did Jane ramble, and invent? Or did she know the truth? Did Jane suffer, as Elizabeth, believing herself deceived, had suffered? How could she be saved?

The door into the hall was opened by the housekeeper, and the doctor – known to Elizabeth, for he had long attended Jane and little Emily, and Elizabeth had many times conferred with him on the subject of the health of her sister and her niece – came in from outside. Then another door – into the sitting-room – also opened. Mr Bingley, accompanied by Mr Darcy, came out.

"Jane has accepted the boy," said Mr Bingley. "She is conscious and coherent sometimes, and she wishes you to know this, Darcy. She is the sweetest angel I have ever had the privilege to spend time with here on earth – "

"She will not die!" cried Elizabeth, for she could not bear these words. She ran – as the three men looked up at her – to come down the stairs, from the landing. Her thoughts were clear, and radiant. Mr Darcy had been much misunderstood. Mr Gresham had misinformed her absolutely – or rather, as she must confess, she had prised information from him that he had never once tried to give. She had been more than prejudiced, in her reaction to the affair: she had been blind. The child was Bingley's, and Darcy had wished only, in those days when he had so eagerly tried to persuade Elizabeth of his conviction that Jane did not love his friend, to save her sister from an unhappy alliance. Once they were wed, he took care of Bingley's child with the Frenchwoman, in the village, and spared Jane the suffering Elizabeth had so foolishly, in her invented case against her own husband, assumed.

Elizabeth, in her haste – for she must show Darcy now that she understood his actions, that she must be the one to beg forgiveness from *him* – slipped on the topmost stair, and fell. She knew nothing more, for all was blackness. When she woke, it was to find the doctor at one side of her, and Darcy at the other.

"You are never to leave me again, do you hear me, Eliza," said Darcy – but in a rough voice that was scarcely audible to her. "You are too precious to me – loveliest Elizabeth, forgive my stupid pride, in abandoning you! Please do so!"

Elizabeth found no breath to reply; but she looked up at Mr Darcy with eyes so fine, smiling and full of love, that Mr Darcy knew he had the answer.

"Mrs Darcy was fortunate in the way she fell," said the doctor as he rose from his examination, "for she is unharmed. And she needs only a day or so at home in bed, to recover completely."

The look which then passed between Mr Darcy and Elizabeth ended only when Charles Bingley came down the stairs from his wife's bedchamber. "She sits up! She has colour! She says, dear Elizabeth, that your visit has returned her to health!"

The doctor soon was able to confirm the improvement in Mrs Bingley; and plans were made for Charles and Jane to visit Pemberley when she was fully recovered, in the way all four truly enjoyed – with no one else in the house but themselves.

That soon there would be an addition to the Darcy family was not told to the Bingleys until they had been several days at Pemberley, in the finest May weather; for Elizabeth and Darcy had so much to talk about, that they liked to keep their secret between them, for a while. Though one secret Elizabeth *did* keep from him: that Dr Carr at Longbourn had suspected she was with child; and that it was with all the agony of this dilemma that she had travelled north to her sister's bedside. That Mrs Bennet and Lady de Bourgh would soon be acquainted of the happy news, and demanding they visit Pemberley in August when the garden was at its finest, could not be doubted at all. Mr Darcy, however, assured his wife that Miss Caroline Bingley would on no account be included in any future invitation to Pemberley; and gravely exacted a promise from *her* that no prospective suitors of Mrs Bennet would be permitted access.

An artist should also be commissioned – so Mr Darcy insisted, even though Elizabeth felt alarmed at the prospect – to paint the portrait of Jane Bingley in a white dress with green ornaments, and Elizabeth Darcy in yellow.